THE OFFICIAL COOKBOOK

THE OFFICIAL COOKBOOK

By Chelsea Monroe-Cassel

INSIGHT ◉ EDITIONS

San Rafael, California

CONTENTS

MAINS
THE WAY OF THE ENTRÉE

DESSERTS
THE WAY OF THE SWEET

DRINKS
THE WAY OF THE TANKARD

NOTE FROM THE AUTHOR

The difficulty with creating real recipes for fictional dishes lies in the world-building. Sometimes a world is not rich enough—not fully imagined enough—to provide adequate details about the foods. In those cases, a stew is just a stew, and bread is just plain old boring bread, no matter how sustaining.

But then there are fictional realms that are so inventive, so creative and unique, that they are instantly immersive. The world of Warcraft is just such a place, where fish both common and rare can be caught in countless bodies of water, where the farmers of Pandaria battle virmen that threaten their crops of enormous vegetables, and where an unusually high number of nonplayer characters need help collecting ingredients for recipes both delicious and dodgy.

And while a lack of details can prove problematic, so too can having such a wealth of them. Cooking mythological creatures is all well and good when sitting in front of a computer, but when it comes to bringing that recipe to life in the kitchen? Well . . . let's just say it can get complicated.

In creating this cookbook, I've tried to keep things relatively simple while staying as true as possible to the dishes and recipes within the game. I hope you'll find some of your old favorites—and perhaps discover a few new ones, too.

Here's hoping you all stay Well Fed on your journey through this book!

—CHELSEA MONROE-CASSEL

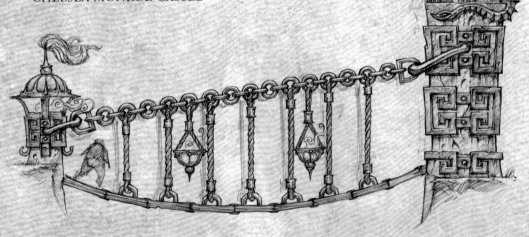

COOKING AZEROTHIAN FOODS

The trick to cooking Azerothian cuisine is learning to build a proper cooking fire. Start with some kindling and twigs and then . . . What?

Oh. You want to cook these dishes in your oven at home? Well, I suppose that's reasonable. More than reasonable, really, given that these recipes started as items in a game; it's only natural that some amount of adjustment was bound to happen during their transformation into real food. In that case, just swing by your local market for some fresh Chimaerok Chops, then take your giant wheelbarrow to the Auction House for a Juicycrunch Carrot, so you can . . . Why are you looking at me like that?

Wait. What do you mean there are no chimaeroks in your world? Seriously, why did you even buy this cookbook if the recipes all rely on ingredients that are imaginary?

Don't worry. The very reason that you can already imagine what these fictional dishes taste like is because the foods of Azeroth have a basis in our own reality. Just because we are using nonimaginary ingredients and a modern kitchen doesn't mean we have to settle for anything less than delicious cuisine that evokes the aesthetic of *World of Warcraft*. The right spices, peppers, salts, vegetables, and meat can make the difference between a dish that leaves a lot to be imagined and one that just might convince you that you're on the plains of Mulgore after all. If you have access to game meat, great! Want the Lukewarm Yak Roast Broth to taste more unique? Go for some bison meat. New recipes are a perfect excuse to try something you've never had before, so go on a quest through your local market.

Despite the impressive globalization of foodstuffs in the modern world, good spices remain one of those items that have retained just a hint of the exotic. Nothing beats a whiff of warm fresh cinnamon or the cool peppery bite of juniper berry. Spices have been treasured throughout the ages, and that connection with history remains with them, giving dishes a richer feeling of authenticity. Don't be a kitchen noob. Level up your seasoning collection: If you've been hoarding the same bottle of ground cinnamon for the last decade, it's probably time to bin it in favor of some fresh stuff. Experiment with interesting new peppers or various types of salt. It's an adventure that will likely end with some really tasty foods.

DIETARY RESTRICTIONS

In this day and age, many of us either struggle with our own dietary restrictions and sensitivities or cook for someone who does. As I am not proficient in cooking with such restrictions, I suspect that, in many of these cases, you will know more about the subject than I ever could.

In the back of this book is a helpful list of all the recipes covered, organized into sections for vegetarian, vegan, and gluten-free cooking. In addition, a number of recipes are marked to indicate that, with a few small changes, they can be made to fit one of those categories. Here are a few guidelines to help you customize the recipes in this book into something you can enjoy worry-free.

ADAPTING TO VEGETARIAN DIETS

While there are many recipes in this book suited to a vegetarian lifestyle, there are also a number that can be adapted for a vegetarian diet.

Depending on the recipe, the change might be as simple as swapping the chicken broth for a vegetable- or mushroom-based broth. Love the sound of a sauce that's meant to go over a piece of meat? Pour it over your favorite meat-substitute or grilled vegetables instead.

ADAPTING TO GLUTEN-FREE DIETS

A wide array of gluten-free flour mixes is commercially available both online and in many grocery shops, and these have been exhaustively tested to perform as well as possible in both baking and cooking. Here are some basic guidelines:

Breads: These can be among the trickiest recipes to adapt for a GF lifestyle. Generally, I would recommend adding what makes the loaf unique to your favorite GF bread recipe, as with the recipes for Mulgore Spice Bread and Kaldorei Pine Nut Bread. Or, in the case of Soft Banana Bread or Sweet Potato Bread, try substituting a one-to-one GF flour for the regular versions in the recipes.

Thickening: If a small amount of flour is included in a recipe as a thickening agent, try substituting cornstarch, rice flour, or your favorite GF flour mix.

Above all, don't be afraid to experiment. Even if you don't need to change anything for a dietary concern, feel free to toy with the ingredients lists. The best recipe in the world is still just a starting point, so adapt to your own tastes and inspirations. Play, eat, enjoy!

ACHIEVEMENTS

To master the fusions of flavors, an adventurer must have dedication, patience, and the willingness to try unusual recipes. Undertake the following to become a Master Cook.

LEVELING UP AS A COOK—

Level up by making 5 dishes from each path. Start out with an apprentice-level recipe and work your way up to the master-level recipes.

1) Make 5 from each:

The Way of the Nibble

The Way of the Loaf

The Way of the Broth

The Way of the Entrée

The Way of the Sweet

The Way of the Tankard

2) You are now a Master Cook.
Go forth and feed the masses!

SPICES AND BASICS

ANCIENT PANDAREN SPICES

SKILL LEVEL: Apprentice
PREP: 5 minutes
MAKES: About ¼ cup

These spices have been a staple ingredient in pandaren recipes for millennia, since before the time of Emperor Shaohao. The unique blend of ingredients will bring that history right to your kitchen.

2 teaspoons Szechuan peppercorns

1 teaspoon fennel seeds

1 teaspoon ground cinnamon

½ teaspoon ground anise

½ teaspoon ground cloves

½ teaspoon ground cardamom

1. **Place all the spices in a dry pan** and gently toast them over medium heat for several minutes. Swirl the pan occasionally to keep the mixture from burning. Once the spices are giving off a lovely fragrance and have darkened slightly, remove from heat and allow to cool.

2. **Transfer the mixture into a spice grinder** or coffee grinder and process until you have a fine powder. Store in a small airtight jar out of direct sunlight. This mix will keep for several months but is at its best when fresh.

Used in:

Spiced Blossom Soup *(page 103)*

Pomfruit Slices *(page 181)*

Rice Pudding *(page 185)*

AUTUMNAL HERBS

SKILL LEVEL: Apprentice
PREP: 5 minutes
MAKES: About ¼ cup

As the days grow short and chilly, our thoughts often turn to time with friends and family and occasions best marked with feasts. This herb mixture is a favorite of Stormwind chefs as they prepare vast meals to celebrate the harvest during Pilgrim's Bounty.

2 tablespoons dried rosemary

2 teaspoons dried thyme

1 teaspoon dried marjoram

½ teaspoon ground cinnamon

¼ teaspoon ground nutmeg

¼ teaspoon ground ginger

1 teaspoon blue cornflower petals (optional)

Combine all spices except the petals and run through a spice grinder or a coffee grinder until there are no large pieces remaining. Add in the petals, and store in an airtight jar.

Used in:
Candied Sweet Potatoes *(page 31)*
Slow-Roasted Turkey *(page 141)*

HOLIDAY SPICES

SKILL LEVEL: Apprentice
PREP: 5 minutes
MAKES: About ¼ cup

With all the warmth and flavor imbued by these spices, an ordinary dish gets a little boost of holiday cheer for the Feast of Winter Veil. You'll need these spices to whip up Greatfather Winter's favorite treats for his yearly visit.

1 tablespoon ground ginger

1 tablespoon ground cinnamon

1 tablespoon ground nutmeg

½ tablespoon ground cloves

¼ tablespoon ground pepper

Combine spices and store in an airtight container.

Used in:
Gingerbread Cookies *(page 169)*
Pumpkin Pie *(page 183)*
Hot Apple Cider *(page 202)*

NORTHERN SPICES

SKILL LEVEL: Apprentice
PREP: 5 minutes
MAKES: About ¼ cup

This aromatic blend of spices will not only increase the flavor of any given recipe but also add a warming element to dishes. That warmth is a welcome addition in the chilly region of Northrend, from which these delicious spices are traditionally gathered.

1 tablespoon cardamom

1 tablespoon dried juniper berries

1 teaspoon smoked salt

½ teaspoon pepper

½ teaspoon ginger

¼ teaspoon allspice or nutmeg

Combine spices and run through a spice grinder or a coffee grinder until there are no large pieces remaining. Store in an airtight jar.

Used in:
Tracker Snacks *(page 59)*
Steaming Chicken Soup *(page 105)*
Firecracker Salmon *(page 123)*
Tender Shoveltusk Steak *(page 143)*

WHIPPED CREAM

SKILL LEVEL: Apprentice
PREP: 5 minutes
MAKES: About 4 cups

Whip the cream to soft peaks using an electric mixer for about 3 minutes.
Add the sugar and any other flavorings listed below, by recipe, and whip those
in by hand.

For the Pumpkin Pie:
Substitute brown sugar for regular sugar.

For the Sugar-Dusted Choux Twists, add:
½ teaspoon ground cardamom
½ teaspoon orange-blossom water

For the Chocolate Celebration Cake, add:
½ cup Nutella, or other hazelnut spread, softened
2 tablespoons cocoa powder
Pinch of ground cinnamon

INGREDIENTS FOR BASIC:

1 pint whipping cream

1 to 2 tablespoons white sugar

Dash of vanilla

Used in:
Chocolate Celebration Cake *(page 153)*
Pumpkin Pie *(page 183)*
Sugar-Dusted Choux Twists *(page 189)*

ROYAL ICING FOR COOKIES

SKILL LEVEL: Apprentice
PREP: 10 minutes
MAKES: 2 cups, enough for
one batch of cookies

Beat all ingredients at low speed for 7 to 10 minutes,
or until icing forms peaks.

Tip: After beating, keep icing covered with a wet kitchen
towel as it can dry out quickly.

Used in:
Chocolate Cookies *(page 155)*
Gingerbread Cookies *(page 169)*

COOK'S NOTE: To make enough for both cookie recipes,
double the ingredients.

2 cups sifted confectioners' sugar

2½ tablespoons water

1½ tablespoons meringue powder

Food coloring, as needed

DRIZZLED ICING & GLAZE

SKILL LEVEL: Apprentice

PREP: 5 minutes

MAKES: About 1 cup

Combine the confectioners' sugar and vanilla, then gradually add the milk, stirring vigorously to eliminate any lumps. Aim for a thick, smooth consistency that you can still drizzle.

For the Rylak Claws:
Add 1 tablespoon honey and reduce milk to 1 to 2 tablespoons.

For the Sugar-Dusted Choux Twists:
Leave out the vanilla. Add 2 teaspoons runny honey—warm up if necessary.

For the Conjured Mana Strudel:
Replace the milk with heavy cream, which will give the icing more body.

1 cup confectioners' sugar

Dash of vanilla

2 to 3 tablespoons milk

Used in:
Conjured Mana Strudel *(page 159)*
Rylak Claws *(page 187)*
Sugar-Dusted Choux Twists *(page 189)*

FLAKY PIE DOUGH

SKILL LEVEL: Apprentice

PREP: 15 minutes

CHILLING: 30 minutes

MAKES: 1 batch

1. **Divide the butter in half.** In a medium-sized bowl, rub half the butter into the flour until you have small pieces of butter the size of peas. Using your palm, press the other half of the butter pieces into flat flakes, and add them to the bowl. Add the water, gently mixing until you have a mostly cohesive dough. Form into a flat round, wrap in plastic, and chill for 30 minutes.

2. **Take out the chilled dough and set it on a lightly floured surface.** Sprinkle a little extra flour on top and roll it out into a long rectangle. Fold the dough into thirds, then rotate, roll out into another long rectangle, and fold into thirds again; this will make your dough flaky and light. Roll out one last time to a smaller rectangle, cut into two equal pieces, wrap in plastic, and chill until ready to use.

2¼ cups flour

1 stick cold, salted butter, cut into large chunks

¼ cup water

Used in:
Graccu's Homemade Meat Pie *(page 127)*
Bloodberry Tart *(page 149)*
Cheery Cherry Pie *(page 151)*
Pumpkin Pie *(page 183)*

BUTTERY PASTRY DOUGH

SKILL LEVEL: Apprentice

PREP: 15 minutes

CHILLING: 6 hours

MAKES: 20 Rylak Claws,
2 strudels, or
20 croissants

1. **In a large bowl, combine the warm water, yeast, and a pinch of the sugar.** Let sit for a few minutes until the yeast has started to bloom.

2. **Meanwhile, add the flour, pieces of butter, and salt to a food processor.** Pulse until the pieces of butter are roughly the size of beans.

3. **Add the rest of the sugar, 2 eggs, and heavy cream to the bowl with the yeast,** stirring vigorously to combine. Gradually add in the flour and butter mixture, working until the mixture just comes together. Divide in half, press the dough into two round discs, wrap with plastic, and chill for at least 6 hours. The chilled dough will keep for several days if well wrapped.

4. **Working with one chilled disc of dough at a time,** transfer to a lightly floured surface, dusting both sides of the dough with extra flour as needed. Using a rolling pin, beat and roll the dough into a long, flat rectangle. Fold both edges over like a letter, making three layers of dough. Roll flat, then rotate the dough and repeat the folding and rolling. Rewrap and return to the fridge to chill until needed. Dough can also be frozen at this stage until needed.

COOK'S NOTE: This dough bakes up rich and flaky, buttery to the taste, and oh-so-delicious. Because the batch of dough is so large, consider splitting it in half and trying two different recipes!

½ cup warm water

2 teaspoons active dry yeast

¼ cup white sugar

2 eggs, plus 1 egg for glazing

½ cup heavy cream

3½ cups all-purpose flour, plus more for dusting

1 cup (2 sticks) salted butter, cold, cut into pieces

½ teaspoon salt

Used in:

Conjured Croissants *(page 67)*

Conjured Mana Strudel *(page 159)*

Rylak Claws *(page 187)*

SIDES

THE WAY OF THE NIBBLE

BOILED CLAMS

SKILL LEVEL: Apprentice

PREP: 5 minutes

COOKING: 5 to 7 minutes

MAKES: 2 to 4 small
   servings

PAIRS WELL WITH: Crusty
   Flatbread (page 71),
   pasta in cream sauce

*Don't be fooled by the simplicity of this dish. Its bites of
tender clam meat will bring the delightful flavors of the
Westfall coast right to your home table.*

3 tablespoons butter

3 cloves garlic, minced

½ cup white wine or light beer

1 pound small clams, rinsed

1 tablespoon minced fresh parsley

**Melt the butter in a medium saucepan over medium heat
and add the garlic,** cooking for a few minutes until just
starting to brown. Pour in the wine or beer and increase heat
to medium-high. Once the mixture is simmering, add the
clams and cover. Simmer for 5 to 7 minutes, during which
time the clams should pop open. Remove from heat and
swirl in the parsley. Transfer the clams and broth to serving
bowls, and enjoy with a large hunk of crusty bread to soak
up all the juicy goodness.

BUZZARD BITES

SKILL LEVEL: Apprentice

PREP: 20 minutes

BAKING: 20 minutes

MAKES: About 2 dozen small meatballs

PAIRS WELL WITH: Cheesy garlic pasta, Hot Apple Cider (page 202)

BAM! The sweet and tangy sauce that covers these bite-sized morsels will make you pucker up and take notice. Combine that with the savory bacon bits scattered throughout, and you've got yourself a snack that goes down smooth as butter.

1 pound ground turkey

½ cup bread crumbs

½ heaping cup crumbled bacon

1 egg

2 tablespoons onion powder

2 tablespoons garlic powder

SAUCE

1½ cups apple cider

1 cup ketchup

½ cup balsamic vinegar

Generous pinch each salt, pepper, and nutmeg

1. **Preheat the oven to 375°F** and line a baking sheet with parchment paper.

2. **Combine all the ingredients in a large bowl and mix until evenly distributed**—hands are the best tool for this. Form into small meatballs, roughly the size of a golf ball, and place on the prepared baking sheet, spacing about 1½ inches apart. Bake for 18 to 20 minutes, until no longer pink in the middle.

3. **While the bites are baking, make the sauce.**

SAUCE: Combine all ingredients in a saucepan and simmer for about 30 minutes, or until it has thickened somewhat. Remove from heat and add the meatballs, stirring and turning to make sure they are all covered. Serve warm.

CANDIED SWEET POTATOES

SKILL LEVEL: Master

PREP: 40 minutes

BAKING: 15 minutes

MAKES: 6 to 8 servings

PAIRS WELL WITH:
Slow-Roasted Turkey
(page 141)

With little clouds of maple-sweetened marshmallow meringue dotting the top, this dish is sure to be a crowd-pleaser. Savory and just the right amount of sweet, this hearty side is our favorite part of the Pilgrim's Bounty meal.

4 large sweet potatoes

6 tablespoons melted butter

4 tablespoons honey

1 teaspoon Autumnal Herbs (page 18)

2 tablespoons brown sugar

MARSHMALLOW MERINGUE

2 egg whites

¼ cup maple syrup

1 cup marshmallow fluff

1. **In a large pot, boil the sweet potatoes until tender when stuck with a fork,** anywhere from 20 to 40 minutes, depending on the size of your sweet potatoes. Remove from heat, allow to cool enough to handle, then peel. Slice into ¼-inch slices, and arrange in a 9 x 12-inch baking dish.

2. **Preheat the oven to 400°F.** Mix together the melted butter, honey, and Autumnal Herbs. Pour this over the sweet potatoes, then sprinkle with brown sugar. Bake for about 10 minutes and prepare the meringue topping while it bakes. When the 10 minutes are up, remove from oven, pipe on dollops of meringue, and return to the oven for another 5 minutes, or until the meringue just starts to brown.

MARSHMALLOW MERINGUE: Beat egg whites to stiff peaks, about 5 minutes. Add the syrup and fluff, and beat again until just mixed. Transfer the mixture to a piping bag with a large tip.

CRAB CAKES

SKILL LEVEL: Expert

PREP: 10 minutes

COOKING: 20 minutes

MAKES: 10 small crab cakes

PAIRS WELL WITH:
Fresh green salad, Fel
Eggs and Ham (page 39)

With such a wide variety of crawler species on the coasts of Azeroth, it's no wonder that some of them end up being served by innkeepers around the world. With just the barest hint of spiciness, these tender Crab Cakes bring the delicious flavor of the seas right to your table.

1 tablespoon salted butter

2 shallots, minced

2 garlic cloves, minced

14 ounces crabmeat

1 cup fresh bread crumbs

2 tablespoons mayonnaise

1 egg

2 tablespoons heavy cream

1 tablespoon flour

½ teaspoon red pepper flakes

1 heaping tablespoon minced parsley

Salt and pepper, to taste

Canola oil for frying

Citrus slices, for serving

1. **Melt the butter in a frying pan over medium-low heat.** Add the shallots and garlic and cook until soft and fragrant, but not too brown. Remove from heat and transfer to a food processor along with all the remaining ingredients except the canola oil. Pulse several times until no large chunks of crabmeat remain. Scoop out a small handful of the mixture and form into a flat patty; if the mix doesn't hold together well, add more cream or flour as needed.

2. **Heat a thin layer of oil in a frying pan** and gently lower several of the crab cakes in. Cook for about 3 minutes, or until the crab cakes are a nice golden color, then flip and cook for another three minutes on the other side. Repeat with the remaining crab cakes. Serve with citrus slices.

CRANBERRY CHUTNEY

SKILL LEVEL: Apprentice

COOKING: 35 to 40 minutes

MAKES: About 4 cups of sauce

PAIRS WELL WITH: Slow-Roasted Turkey (page 141), a cheese plate, savory sandwiches

Originally published in the *Bountiful Cookbook*, this traditional Pilgrim's Bounty recipe was previously unavailable outside Azeroth. With a nice balance between the sweetness of the honey and the tart pop of the berries, this versatile and simple-to-make condiment will please family, guests, and partygoers alike.

1 small onion, diced

1 clove garlic, minced

1 tablespoon minced candied ginger

½ cup apple cider vinegar

½ cup honey

⅓ cup port

1 to 2 tablespoons balsamic vinegar

1 clove, pressed

½ teaspoon each cinnamon, ground coriander, pepper

Pinch each mace or nutmeg, ground cloves, salt

1 pear, cored and diced

1 apple, cored and diced

One 12-ounce bag fresh cranberries

1. **In a large saucepan, combine all the ingredients except the pear, apple, and cranberries.** Simmer for about 5 minutes over medium-high heat.

2. **Add the pear and apple, cooking for another 5 minutes until the fruit is soft but not falling apart.** Reduce the heat to medium and add the cranberries. Cook for another 15 to 20 minutes until the cranberries have popped open and the whole mixture has the consistency of a thick jam.

3. **Keep refrigerated** but allow to come to room temperature before serving.

CRISPY BAT WINGS

SKILL LEVEL: Apprentice

PREP: 10 minutes

BAKING: 1½ hours

MAKES: 2 to 4 servings

PAIRS WELL WITH: Beer, beans, rice, Honey-Spiced Lichen (page 43), Pandaren Plum Wine (page 206)

Based on Abigail Shiel's famous recipe, this Undercity snack is a favorite among the Horde. Every tender bite of this crispy, flavorful dish—whether made with proper bat meat or with chicken as a substitute—will satisfy any adventurer's cravings.

2 pounds chicken wings

¼ cup baking powder

¾ teaspoon salt

1 tablespoon blackberry jelly

2 tablespoons soy sauce

1 teaspoon Sriracha sauce

1. **Preheat the oven to 250°F.** Line a baking sheet with foil and place a lightly oiled cooling rack atop that, which will allow the wings to cook more evenly. Rinse the wings and pat them dry. Combine the baking powder and salt, then dip the dried wings into the mixture. Brush off any excess, then place on the rack.

2. **Begin by baking at 250°F for 25 minutes,** then increase the heat to 400°F. Bake for an additional 40 minutes, or until the wings have begun to turn a nice light golden brown.

3. **While the wings cook, make the glaze** by combining the jelly, soy sauce, and Sriracha sauce.

4. **When the wings are done, remove from oven and brush on the glaze.** Return to oven for a final 5 minutes. Allow to cool slightly before serving.

FEL EGGS AND HAM

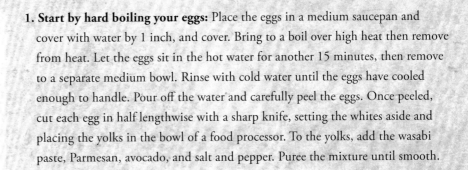

SKILL LEVEL: Master

PREP: 30 minutes

MAKES: 1 dozen deviled eggs

PAIRS WELL WITH:
Crab Cakes (page 33), assorted sharp cheeses

You can eat them near or far; you can eat them in Orgrimmar! Far less dangerous to make than its wild counterpart, this version of Fel Eggs and Ham will have you saying, "Yes! I DO like this!" Simple but flavorful, the creamy filling is topped by a crisp, salty piece of prosciutto, making for a presentation that is as stealthily impressive as it is tasty.

6 eggs

½ teaspoon wasabi paste

¼ cup Parmesan cheese

1 avocado, pitted and peeled

Salt and pepper to taste

2 tablespoons olive oil, divided

3 thin slices prosciutto

1. **Start by hard boiling your eggs:** Place the eggs in a medium saucepan and cover with water by 1 inch, and cover. Bring to a boil over high heat then remove from heat. Let the eggs sit in the hot water for another 15 minutes, then remove to a separate medium bowl. Rinse with cold water until the eggs have cooled enough to handle. Pour off the water and carefully peel the eggs. Once peeled, cut each egg in half lengthwise with a sharp knife, setting the whites aside and placing the yolks in the bowl of a food processor. To the yolks, add the wasabi paste, Parmesan, avocado, and salt and pepper. Puree the mixture until smooth.

2. **You can either fill each half egg white with this mixture by spoon or by piping it in.** If piping, use a very large tip, or no tip at all, to prevent clogging. Set the filling aside while you make the prosciutto flakes. If making the filling ahead of time, be sure to cover tightly with plastic, as exposure to the air will discolor it.

3. **Heat 1 tablespoon of the olive oil in a pan over medium heat,** and tear the prosciutto into pieces roughly the size of a half dollar; don't worry if you have irregular pieces left over; they will still be delicious! Gently fry the prosciutto in the hot oil for several minutes, flipping once, until both sides are darker and crispy. Remove the finished pieces to a plate lined with paper towel to drain.

4. **Place a piece of crispy prosciutto on top of each filled egg white and serve immediately;** if left to sit too long, the filling will darken and the prosciutto will soften.

HERB-BAKED EGGS

SKILL LEVEL: Expert

PREP: 10 minutes

BAKING: About 10 minutes

SERVES: 2

PAIRS WELL WITH:
Breakfast tea or strong coffee

Quick, fairly easy, and great practice for chefs looking to level up their cooking. This recipe produces a delicious breakfast that will have you fed and ready to face whatever adventures, quests, or battles come your way.

Pinch each fresh thyme, rosemary, and parsley, minced

1 tablespoon grated Parmesan cheese

Pinch each salt and pepper

4 eggs

2 tablespoons heavy cream

1 tablespoon unsalted butter

Toasted bread cut into strips, for serving

1. **Preheat the broiler on high** and move a rack up near the top of the oven, just under the heat.

2. **The trick to this recipe is having everything ready when you start:** Combine the herbs, Parmesan cheese, and the salt and pepper in a small bowl. Crack the eggs into small bowls or teacups, two in each; this will enable you to quickly pour them into the baking dishes.

3. **Place two small oven-safe dishes onto a baking sheet.** Divide the butter and cream equally between the dishes, and place these under the broiler. Cook for about 2 to 3 minutes, until the mixture is hot and bubbling. Quickly remove the pan from the oven, then tip two eggs into each hot dish. Sprinkle liberally with the herb-cheese mixture, then put back under the broiler for another 3 to 5 minutes. When the whites of the eggs are just about cooked through, remove from the oven. Allow the dishes to sit for an additional minute to finish cooking, then carefully transfer to a heatproof plate or an oven mitt.

4. **Serve immediately with strips of toast,** and take care while eating, as the dishes will still be quite hot.

HONEY-SPICED LICHEN

SKILL LEVEL: Apprentice

PREP: 5 minutes

COOKING: 50 minutes

MAKES: About 4 small servings

PAIRS WELL WITH: Crispy Bat Wings (page 37), dry white wine, your favorite dipping sauce

With just a dash of sweetness, these crunchy "lichen" crisps are a tasty way to enjoy daily greens. Often peddled by fungus vendors, these highly nutritious snacks of the Undercity undead are now easy to make yourself.

4 to 6 large kale leaves

2 tablespoons honey

2 tablespoons olive oil

¼ teaspoon garlic powder

Pinch of cayenne pepper

1. **Preheat the oven to 200°F** and line a baking sheet with parchment paper. Tear the kale into pieces about 2 inches across, discarding any large pieces of stem. In a medium bowl, combine the honey, olive oil, and spices. Toss the kale in this mixture, making sure that each leaf is covered completely, then allow any excess to drip off. Lay the kale on the prepared baking sheet, arranging so that the pieces are touching as little as possible. Bake for about 50 minutes, flipping the kale once halfway through, until the pieces are crisp and flaky. Remove from heat, allow to cool, and enjoy.

SAUTÉED CARROTS

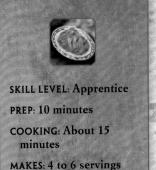

SKILL LEVEL: Apprentice

PREP: 10 minutes

COOKING: About 15 minutes

MAKES: 4 to 6 servings

PAIRS WELL WITH: Winter Veil Roast (page 145)

This might be the simplest of the closely guarded recipes taught by Anthea Ironpaw, Master of the Wok, but it's no less delicious than the others. Tender carrots are coated with a sweet and savory glaze, topped with just a slight zing of ginger.

1 pound carrots, peeled, and cut into sticks about 3 inches long

2 tablespoons unsalted butter

1 tablespoon soy sauce

1 tablespoon honey

1 tablespoon minced fresh ginger

1. **Bring a large saucepan of salted water to a boil.** Add the carrots and cook until tender, about 8 minutes, then remove from heat and drain.

2. **In a large skillet over medium-low heat, melt the butter.** Stir in the carrots and soy sauce and cook over high heat until the carrots are browned in spots, 2 minutes. Stir in the honey and ginger, and cook until the carrots are glazed, 2 minutes longer. Transfer to a platter and serve.

SLICED ZANGAR BUTTONS

SKILL LEVEL: Apprentice

PREP: 5 minutes

COOKING: 20 minutes

MAKES: 2 to 4 servings

PAIRS WELL WITH: Tender Shoveltusk Steak (page 143), rustic bread

Traditionally crafted using thin shavings of the enormous fungi of Zangarmarsh, this savory dish has been adapted to work with more common varieties of mushrooms. Despite the small change, it remains a flavorful accompaniment to any main course.

3 tablespoons unsalted butter, divided

1 tablespoon extra-virgin olive oil

10 ounces button mushrooms, cleaned and sliced

1 clove garlic, minced

Salt and pepper to taste

1 teaspoon dried thyme (or ½ tablespoon fresh)

2 tablespoons flour

1½ cups beef stock

1 tablespoon Worcestershire sauce

1. **Melt 2 tablespoons of the butter and the olive oil in a medium frying pan over medium-high heat.** Add the sliced mushrooms and carefully stir. Cook for several minutes, until the mushrooms have absorbed most of the butter and have shrunk down some.

2. **Make a small well in the middle of the pan,** and add the remaining butter and minced garlic, followed by the salt, pepper, and thyme. Continue to stir for another 10 minutes or so, during which time the mushroom will put off a lot of liquid. Cook off most of that liquid, then dust with the flour, stirring until there are no visible clumps left. Add the stock and Worcestershire sauce, and cook for five more minutes until the gravy has thickened. Remove from heat and serve.

SOUR GOAT CHEESE

SKILL LEVEL: Expert

PREP: 15 minutes

DRAINING: 2 to 12 hours

MAKES: 1 cup

PAIRS WELL WITH:
  Crusty Flatbread (page 71), apple slices

Nothing beats a nice tart, creamy goat cheese, and you'll hear no argument about that from Jaina Proudmoore, who considers this one of her favorite snacks. Delicious on its own or with savory herbs mixed in, it's just the thing to enjoy while curled up with a good scroll.

1 quart goat milk

Juice of 2 lemons, or ¼ cup apple cider vinegar

Salt, to taste

Finely chopped fresh herbs, like parsley, sage, chives, etc.

1. **Line a strainer with several layers of cheesecloth,** and set over a medium-sized bowl.

2. **Pour the goat milk into a medium saucepan,** and bring up to 180°F. Remove the pan from heat and stir in the lemon juice. The milk should begin to separate into cloudy whorls. Pour the milk through the cheesecloth, letting the bowl underneath catch the liquid, and the cheesecloth the solids. Once most of the liquid has drained through, tie the cheesecloth up into a little bundle and hang over the bowl for 2 hours, minimum. If you'd like your cheese to have more body, hang overnight.

3. **When ready, unwrap the cheese into a small bowl.** Work in the salt, and any herbs you might like. Form into a ball or a log, and wrap tightly to keep fresh for up to a week.

SPICE BREAD STUFFING

SKILL LEVEL: Apprentice

PREP: 15 minutes

BAKING: 45 minutes

MAKES: 8 to 10 servings

PAIRS WELL WITH:
  Slow-Roasted Turkey
  (page 141)

What better accompaniment to a fine celebration of the season's bounty than a heaping helping of stuffing alongside a generous slice of turkey?

1 loaf of Mulgore Spice Bread (page 83), or 8 to 10 cups large bread cubes

2 ½ cups milk

½ cup salted butter

1 onion, diced

1 pear, cored and diced large

1 apple, cored and diced large

1 egg

½ teaspoon salt

2 tablespoons fresh parsley, finely chopped

1 tablespoon fresh sage, minced

1 teaspoon fresh thyme

1. **Cut the bread into chunks no larger than 2 inches wide** and allow to dry out overnight or under low heat in the oven. Transfer the bread into a large mixing bowl. Pour the milk over the bread cubes, stirring until the bread has soaked up all the milk.

2. **In a small frying pan, melt the butter** and cook the onion until it is soft and translucent, about 6 minutes. Add the remaining ingredients to the bowl, tossing until everything is evenly mixed.

3. **Either use the mixture to stuff a turkey or bake in the oven at 350°F,** covered, for about 30 minutes, then another 10 minutes or so uncovered.

SPICED BEEF JERKY

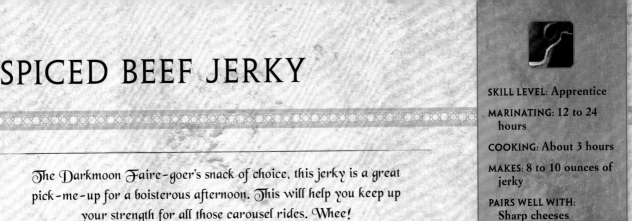

SKILL LEVEL: Apprentice

MARINATING: 12 to 24 hours

COOKING: About 3 hours

MAKES: 8 to 10 ounces of jerky

PAIRS WELL WITH: Sharp cheeses

The Darkmoon Faire-goer's snack of choice, this jerky is a great pick-me-up for a boisterous afternoon. This will help you keep up your strength for all those carousel rides. Whee!

1 pound roast beef, sliced ⅛-inch thick

3 tablespoons soy sauce

3 tablespoons brown sugar

1 teaspoon onion powder

1 teaspoon garlic powder

1 teaspoon sesame oil

1. **Combine all ingredients in an airtight bag and allow to marinate overnight,** or for a full day. Before starting to dehydrate, move the oven racks to the top and bottom positions. Slide a baking sheet lined with aluminum foil onto the bottom rack of the oven to catch drips. Shake any excess marinade off the meat, and hang either from the top oven rack itself or from wooden skewers suspended between the grills of the rack. Heat the oven to 200°F, and allow to the meat to cook for about 3 hours, or until it is sufficiently dried out. Break into pieces and store in a cool place in an airtight container.

SPICY VEGETABLE CHIPS

SKILL LEVEL: Master

PREP: 20 minutes

BAKING: 45 minutes

MAKES: About 4 servings of chips

PAIRS WELL WITH: Cheddar-Beer Dip (page 75)

This pandaren staple is a healthier and more flavorful alternative to ordinary potato chips. With bursts of fiery spice, you'll love each crunchy bite.

1 parsnip

1 carrot

1 medium sweet potato

1 raw beet

2 tablespoons olive oil

¼ teaspoon mild chili powder

½ teaspoon coarse salt, plus more for sprinkling

1. **Preheat oven to 300°F,** and line several baking sheets with parchment paper.

2. **Thinly slice all vegetables using a mandolin slicer or a sharp knife,** and toss with the olive oil, chili, and salt—keep the parsnips and sweet potato separate from the beets so the red color doesn't get all over the other veggies. Let any excess oil drip back into the bowl, then lay the chips out on the baking sheets in a single layer that doesn't overlap too much.

3. **Baking the chips will work best if similar veggies are put on the same baking sheet,** so pair the carrot and parsnip, and give the sweet potato and the beet their own sheets. Bake for about 30 minutes, then check for doneness. The chips should be mostly dry to the touch when done and crispy. Remove chips as they finish baking, and continue to check the rest until the whole batch is finished. Allow to cool before eating, and sprinkle with a little extra salt.

COOK'S NOTE: Many, many vegetables make delicious chips, but the baking times for each may vary. Keep a close eye on them to make sure they don't burn.

STUFFED LUSHROOMS

SKILL LEVEL: Expert

PREP: 20 minutes

COOKING: About 30 minutes

MAKES: 4 to 6 servings, more as a party appetizer

PAIRS WELL WITH: Light beer, Lukewarm Yak Roast Broth (page 101)

Once a favored dish of the ancient mogu, this recipe has become a staple in pandaren cuisine. Packed with flavors and textures that vie for dominance with one another, these tender bite-sized morsels make for an easy–but impressive–appetizer.

10 ounces button mushrooms

1 teaspoon peanut or sesame oil

1 teaspoon minced fresh ginger

1 clove garlic, minced

1 cup ground pork sausage (about 8 ounces)

1 tablespoon soy sauce

½ cup panko breadcrumbs

¼ cup grated Parmesan cheese

1 tablespoon sesame seeds

2 tablespoons scallions, minced

1. **Preheat the oven to 350°F** and lightly grease a baking sheet with oil.

2. **Clean the mushrooms,** then pull the stems from the caps and set aside. Place the caps on the prepared baking sheet, hollow side up. Mince the stems very fine. In a skillet, heat the oil over medium-low heat, then add the ginger and garlic, stirring until lightly brown, no more than 5 minutes. Add the minced mushroom stems, and cook until those are soft, another minute or two. Add the pork sausage, and cook until browned, another 5 minutes or so. Remove from heat and pour off any excess fat from the pan. Pour in the soy sauce, stirring to incorporate it into the mixture.

3. **Transfer to a bowl and allow to cool.** Add the remaining ingredients, making sure they are evenly distributed. Put a little of the filling into the hollow of each mushroom cap, then heap more on top of that, pressing into a little mound. Bake for about 15 minutes. Allow to cool slightly before serving.

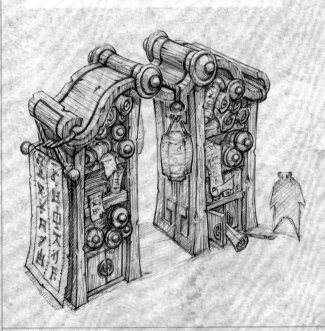

TRACKER SNACKS

SKILL LEVEL: Apprentice

PREP: 10 minutes

COOKING: About 20 minutes

MAKES: 16 to 20 pieces

PAIRS WELL WITH: Chocolate, creamy cheeses, Bean Soup (page 93)

The delicious smell emanating from a hot plate of Tracker Snacks will definitely help you find wayward house pets, but be careful that you don't attract unwanted attention from other beasts.

½ cup light brown sugar

1 tablespoon Northern Spices (page 20)

1 pound thick-sliced bacon

1. **Preheat the oven to 375°F** and line a baking sheet with foil, then set a cooling rack over top of it.

2. **Mix together the brown sugar and the Northern Spices.** Cut the bacon strips in half, then dip each piece in the sugar mix, covering both sides lightly and brushing off any excess. Lay each sugared piece on the rack—if you have too many pieces to fit on one tray, either use a second baking sheet or bake in two rounds.

3. **Bake for about 15 to 20 minutes,** then start checking for doneness. If you like your bacon crispier, bake a little longer. When finished, remove from the oven and gently pat dry to soak up any extra fat on top of the bacon. Allow to cool on the rack, or transfer to a clean plate.

WILD RICE CAKES

SKILL LEVEL: Expert

PREP: 10 minutes

COOKING: 30 minutes

MAKES: About 10 rice cakes

PAIRS WELL WITH: Slow-Roasted Turkey (page 141) or other poultry

Made in the north of Kalimdor according to a traditional night elf recipe, these rice cakes showcase all the healthy, earthy goodness of natural ingredients.

1 tablespoon butter

1 clove garlic, minced

2 small leeks, half-moon cut

½ cup heavy cream

2 cups cooked wild rice

1 egg

½ cup sweet corn, fresh or frozen

¼ cup shelled edamame

¼ cup grated mozzarella cheese

1 teaspoon salt

½ teaspoon black pepper

1½ cups flour

Vegetable oil for frying

1. **Melt the butter in a medium frying pan over medium-low heat,** then cook the garlic and leeks until they are soft but not too brown, about 3 minutes. Pour in the heavy cream, and stir for another minute, until the leeks have absorbed some of the liquid. Remove from heat, transfer to a mixing bowl, and allow to cool. Add in all other ingredients except the flour, mixing thoroughly. Gradually work in the flour until you have a dense dough that isn't too sticky.

2. **Pour just enough oil into a frying pan to cover the bottom,** and heat over medium-low. Using lightly oiled hands, form the rice mixture into patties roughly 5 inches across and ½-inch thick. Working in batches, drop the patties into the hot pan and cook for about three minutes, flipping halfway through, until golden on each side and cooked through.

BREADS

THE WAY OF THE LOAF

BUTTERY WHEAT ROLLS

SKILL LEVEL: Expert

PREP: 20 minutes

RISING: 20 minutes

BAKING: 20 minutes

MAKES: About 20 rolls

PAIRS WELL WITH: Any savory entrée or soup

If you find yourself in need of a soft roll full of sweet, warm, buttery goodness, then look no further. Light and fluffy, these make an excellent pairing with any meal, but especially soups.

2 cups milk, warmed

2 teaspoons sugar

1 tablespoon instant yeast

4 tablespoons salted butter, melted, plus a little more for the tops

1 teaspoon salt

5 cups flour

1. **In a large bowl, combine the milk and sugar,** stirring until the sugar has dissolved. Add the yeast, and let sit for a minute. Add the melted butter and salt, then gradually work in the flour until you have a nice light dough. Turn out onto a floured surface and knead for several minutes, until the dough bounces back when poked.

2. **Preheat the oven to 400°F** and butter an 8 x12 inch-baking pan. Divide the dough in half, then each half into ten balls of dough, pulling the dough around until each ball is smooth and even. Place the rolls in the buttered pan, evenly spaced and just barely touching. Cover and let rise for 20 minutes.

3. **Bake for about 20 minutes,** or until the tops are a nice golden brown. Brush with salted butter and serve warm.

CONJURED CROISSANTS

SKILL LEVEL: Master

PREP: 10 minutes

RISING: 1 hour

BAKING: 15 to 20 minutes

MAKES: About 20 croissants

PAIRS WELL WITH: Your favorite jam or preserves

These flaky, buttery crescents all but melt in your mouth. They are showy rolls for breakfast, tea, or special occasions, and are sure to impress even the grumpiest orc. Make sure to summon extras for hungry and under-prepared adventurers.

1 batch of Buttery Pastry Dough (page 23)

1 egg, beaten

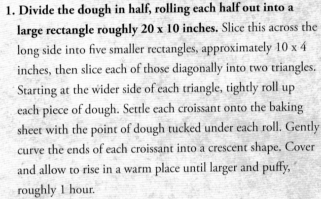

1. **Divide the dough in half, rolling each half out into a large rectangle roughly 20 x 10 inches.** Slice this across the long side into five smaller rectangles, approximately 10 x 4 inches, then slice each of those diagonally into two triangles. Starting at the wider side of each triangle, tightly roll up each piece of dough. Settle each croissant onto the baking sheet with the point of dough tucked under each roll. Gently curve the ends of each croissant into a crescent shape. Cover and allow to rise in a warm place until larger and puffy, roughly 1 hour.

2. **Brush each croissant with the beaten egg.** Bake at 400°F for 15 to 20 minutes, or until a nice golden brown.

CORNMEAL BISCUITS

SKILL LEVEL: Apprentice

PREP: 5 minutes

BAKING: 25 to 30 minutes

MAKES: About a dozen
   biscuits

PAIRS WELL WITH:
   Dragonbreath Chili
   (page 97), butter and
   honey

Once merely a staple food among the tauren tribes in Mulgore, these simple little nuggets of cheesy, buttery flavor have traveled along various trade routes and are now enjoyed in many regions across Azeroth. Enjoy these delicious gems on their own, warm from the oven, or alongside a steaming bowl of chili.

1⅓ cups all-purpose flour

1 cup cornmeal

2½ teaspoons baking powder

½ teaspoon salt

½ cup salted butter

½ cup shredded cheddar cheese

1 cup buttermilk

1. **Preheat the oven to 375°F** and line a baking sheet with parchment paper.

2. **Combine the flour, cornmeal, baking powder, and salt in a medium bowl.** Rub or cut in the butter until no large chunks remain. Add the shredded cheese and toss to distribute evenly, then stir in the buttermilk until the mixture is just moistened.

3. **Drop the mixture onto the prepared baking sheet,** ¼ cup at a time, leaving about 2 inches between each to accommodate spreading as the biscuits bake. Bake for 25 to 30 minutes, or until the tops of the biscuits are golden brown.

CRUSTY FLATBREAD

SKILL LEVEL: Apprentice

PREP: 10 minutes

BAKING: 30 minutes

MAKES: About 4 servings

PAIRS WELL WITH:
Sour Goat Cheese (page 49), jam, hummus, or other dips

Adventuring in Northrend is serious business and requires serious sustenance. Perfect for travel, these crisp little pieces of flatbread have just a hint of herbs and a satisfying crunch.

1¾ cups flour

1 tablespoon fresh rosemary, minced

1 teaspoon baking powder

¾ teaspoon salt

⅓ cup olive oil plus more for brushing

½ cup water

Flaky sea salt

1. **Preheat the oven to 450°F** and place a flat baking sheet on the middle rack.

2. **Mix the dry ingredients and the rosemary in a medium bowl.** Add the oil, and gradually, the water, until you have dough that pulls away from the sides of the bowl. Turn out onto a lightly floured surface and knead for several minutes.

3. **Divide the dough into three parts.** Roll one piece of dough out on a sheet of parchment paper to a disc about 10 inches across. Brush the top of the dough with a little olive oil and sprinkle with some sea salt. Slide the dough, parchment and all, onto the hot baking sheet in the oven. Bake for 8 to 10 minutes, until it is starting to turn golden on top. Allow to cool. Repeat this process with the other two pieces of dough. When the three flatbreads are cool, break into pieces to serve.

ESSENTIAL BREWFEST PRETZELS

SKILL LEVEL: Master

PREP: 15 minutes

RISING: About 1 hour

BAKING: About 12 minutes

MAKES: 10 pretzels

PAIRS WELL WITH: Beer, cheese dip, mustard, honey

Soft and perfectly snackable, these golden pretzels are best enjoyed in the autumn with cheese and booze!

1½ cups warm water

1 tablespoon brown sugar

1 teaspoon salt

2 teaspoons instant yeast

¼ cup butter, melted and cooled

4 cups all-purpose flour

1 egg for glazing, beaten with 1 teaspoon water

Rough salt for sprinkling on top

WATER BATH

10 cups water

⅔ cup baking soda

1. **In a large bowl, combine the water, sugar, salt, and yeast** and allow to sit for a few minutes until the yeast has softened and begun to foam. Add the melted butter, then the flour, a cup at a time, until you have a soft, workable dough that isn't sticky.

2. **Turn the dough out onto a lightly floured surface** and knead for several minutes, until the dough bounces back when poked. Move the dough to a lightly greased bowl, cover lightly with plastic wrap, and set in a warm place to rise for about an hour, or until doubled in bulk.

3. **Meanwhile, bring the 10 cups of water to a boil,** then add the baking soda. Remove from heat and stir until the soda is dissolved. Once the dough has risen, divide it in half, then divide each half into five equal pieces. Working gently with the dough, roll each piece out into a rope about 20 inches long. Fold the rope into a U shape, cross the ends, then bring them back down to meet the curved loop at the bottom of the pretzel. Repeat this process with all the pieces of dough.

4. **Preheat the oven to 400°F** and line two baking sheets with parchment paper. Working one at a time, gently slide each pretzel into the warm baking soda bath. Spoon the warm water over the top of the pretzel for 30 seconds to a minute, during which time the pretzel should start to puff up. Using a spatula (or two), lift the pretzel out of the water and place on the prepared baking sheet. Repeat with the rest of the pretzels, then brush each one with beaten egg and sprinkle with a little salt. Bake for about 12 minutes, or until the pretzels are a nice dark brown.

CHEDDAR-BEER DIP

SKILL LEVEL: Apprentice

COOKING: 15 minutes

MAKES: 1 batch

PAIRS WELL WITH: Essential Brewfest Pretzels (page 73), Spicy Vegetable Chips (page 55)

This Cheddar-Beer Dip is a perfect complement to the Essential Brewfest Pretzels. Be sure to chase down the dip with beer!

2 tablespoons salted butter

2 tablespoons flour

1 cup pale low-hop beer, such as a pilsner

½ cup milk

½ teaspoon mustard

½ teaspoon garlic powder

½ teaspoon paprika

Dash of Worcestershire sauce

3 cups sharp cheddar cheese, shredded

Salt and pepper to taste

1. **In a medium frying pan, melt the butter over medium heat.** Whisk in the flour and cook for a minute or two, until the mixture has turned a nice golden color. While whisking, gradually pour in the beer then the milk, both of which should thicken as they heat. Remove from heat and stir in the spices, Worcestershire sauce, and the cheese. Let the cheese melt; season to taste with salt and pepper.

COOK'S NOTE: For a peppier sauce, try a spicier cheese like a pepperjack. Or, for a creamy, more tangy sauce, add a little goat cheese. Innovate to your tastes!

FRYBREAD

This fast and easy recipe creates a tasty bread that is equally delicious with savory or sweet toppings. Each soft bite entices you to take another, making it a filling side for any meal.

SKILL LEVEL: Apprentice

PREP: 10 minutes

COOKING: 20 minutes

MAKES: 8 frybreads

PAIRS WELL WITH:
Taco toppings, any hot soup, garlic and parmesan or honey

2 cups flour

2 teaspoons baking powder

1 teaspoon salt

¾ cup whole milk, plus more as needed

Vegetable oil for frying

1. **Combine dry ingredients in a medium bowl,** then gradually work in just enough milk to make a soft dough that isn't too sticky. Turn out onto a lightly floured surface and knead for several minutes, until the dough is smooth and bounces back when poked. Divide into 8 equal pieces, and roll each out to about 7 inches across.

2. **In a medium frying pan, heat about 1 inch of oil over medium heat.** Once the oil is hot, begin frying the bread by lowering one piece at a time into the pan. It should puff up and turn golden in a very short amount of time, so keep an eye on it. When one side is done, flip over and fry until the other side is also golden. Move each cooked frybread to a plate lined with paper towel—don't stack the frybreads, as they might get soggy from the oil. If possible, prop the frybreads up on one edge to allow them to drain more fully. Add your favorite toppings and enjoy.

HONEY BREAD

SKILL LEVEL: Master

PREP: 20 minutes

RISING: 1½ hours

BAKING: About 25 minutes

MAKES: 2 small loaves

PAIRS WELL WITH: Butter, jam, honey

Shaped like the hives of the wild bees they have domesticated in Eversong Woods, this blood elven bread does not disappoint. Enjoy it with jam or more honey—because you can't have too much honey.

¼ cup warm water

¾ cup rolled oats

½ cup milk, warmed

2 tablespoons butter, melted

½ cup honey

2 teaspoons instant dry yeast

1½ teaspoons salt

1 egg

Up to 3 cups flour

1. **Combine the warm water and oats in a large bowl,** letting them sit for five minutes to soak. Add the milk, honey, yeast, salt, and one tablespoon of the melted butter to the bowl. Beat in the egg, and then gradually mix in the flour, one cup at a time—you may not need all of it—until you have a nice, workable dough that isn't too sticky. Turn it out onto a lightly floured surface and knead for several minutes until the dough bounces back when poked. Place the dough in a lightly greased bowl and set in a warm place to rise for about an hour, or until doubled in size.

2. **Butter the outside of a small mixing bowl roughly 8 inches wide and 6 inches tall.** Set upside down on a baking sheet. Divide the dough into four equal parts. Roll these pieces of dough out into ropes, each about 3 feet long. Beginning at the top of the overturned bowl, coil one rope around itself, working your way outward and down the bowl. When you reach the end of the first piece, pinch another length of dough onto the end and continue coiling, forming a beehive shape. It's fine if the dough doesn't reach all the way to the baking sheet when you are done—it will expand as it rises. Cover the dough lightly and allow to rise again for about half the time as before.

3. **Preheat the oven to 350°F,** and once the bread has risen again, move the baking sheet to the oven and bake for around 20 minutes, or until the outside of the bread is a light golden color. Brush with the remaining tablespoon of melted butter, and allow to cool before gently lifting the bread off the bowl.

KALDOREI PINE NUT BREAD

SKILL LEVEL: Expert

PREP: 10 minutes

RISING: 1 hour, 15 minutes

BAKING: 15 to 20 minutes

MAKES: 1 large loaf

PAIRS WELL WITH: Pasta dishes, fresh sliced garlic, Steaming Chicken Soup (page 105)

The night elves of Darnassus revere nature, so it is no wonder that their signature bread features ingredients foraged from the forests of Kalimdor: wild hive honey, pine nuts, and mixed herbs. Additionally, it is often formed into the shape of a leaf to honor Teldrassil, the World Tree. Passed down from the night elves' forebears, this ancient recipe makes for a scrumptious accompaniment to pastas and stews.

1½ cups milk, warmed

1 teaspoon honey

2 teaspoons instant yeast

1 egg

4 teaspoons olive oil

½ cup grated Parmesan cheese

1½ teaspoons dried Italian seasoning

¾ teaspoon kosher salt

½ cup pine nuts, roughly chopped

4 cups bread flour

1 egg, beaten, for glaze

1. **Add milk to a large mixing bowl.** Stir the honey into the milk until it has dissolved, and then add the yeast, egg, and olive oil. Add the dry ingredients to the mixture, ending with the flour just a cup or so at a time, until you have a nice pliable dough that starts to pull away from the bowl. Turn it out onto a lightly floured surface and knead for several minutes, until the dough bounces back when poked. Place into a large lightly oiled bowl, cover loosely with plastic wrap, and allow to rise in a warm place for about an hour, or until doubled in size.

2. **Preheat the oven to 400°F,** and line two large baking sheets with parchment. Divide the dough into three equal pieces and, with lightly oiled hands, begin stretching into a leaf shape roughly 1 inch thick, then place on the baking sheet. Using a sharp knife, make several decorative score marks in the dough, cutting all the way through. Gently spread the dough apart to widen the cuts, then let rise for another 15 minutes. Bake for 15 to 20 minutes, until the loaves are a nice golden brown color. Remove from oven and sprinkle with a little extra parmesan and salt if you like. This bread is best when enjoyed the same day.

MULGORE SPICE BREAD

SKILL LEVEL: Expert

PREP: 15 minutes

RISING: 1½ hours

BAKING: 25 minutes

MAKES: 1 loaf

PAIRS WELL WITH: Butter and jam, various nut butters, Roasted Barley Tea (page 208)

Whether you're enjoying this bread on its own, fresh from the oven, or with a dollop of your favorite tauren jam, you'll know right away that this is no ordinary spice bread, but Mulgore spice bread. It's really that good, which is why it's now enjoyed across all of Azeroth.

1½ cups warm milk

2 tablespoons brown sugar

2 teaspoons instant yeast

Mulgore spices (½ teaspoon each ground cardamom, ginger, cinnamon; pinch each ground cloves, mace)

1 teaspoon salt

2 tablespoons butter, melted

3 cups flour

1. **In a medium-sized bowl, combine the warm milk, brown sugar, and the yeast,** and allow to sit for about 5 minutes, until frothy. Add the spices and salt, followed by the butter and half the flour. Gradually add the remaining flour until the dough comes together and pulls away from the side of the bowl.

2. **Tip the dough out onto a lightly floured surface** and knead for a few minutes, until it bounces back when poked. Place in a lightly greased bowl and cover with a tea towel. Allow to rise for about an hour, or until doubled in size. Punch the dough back down.

3. **Preheat the oven to 425°F.** Pulling the sides of the dough, gradually shape it into an oblong loaf. Place this on a sheet of parchment paper on top of a baking sheet, and allow to rise for 30 minutes. Using a sharp knife, slash a few decorative marks on the top of the dough, then bake for about 25 minutes.

RED BEAN BUNS

SKILL LEVEL: Master

PREP: 15 minutes

RISING: 1½ hours

BAKING: 18 to 20 minutes

MAKES: About 10 buns

PAIRS WELL WITH:
Wildfowl Ginseng Soup
(page 111)

These unusual little buns aren't just a pretty addition to a table setting; they are also delicious, packed with a soft, sweet bean filling that makes them difficult to stop eating. No wonder they are Li Li Stormstout's favorite snack!

½ cup milk, warmed

2 tablespoons unsalted butter, melted

2 tablespoons sugar

1 tablespoon instant yeast

1 egg, separated

¼ teaspoon salt

2 cups flour

Half an 18-ounce can of sweetened red bean paste

1 teaspoon sesame seeds or poppy seeds

1. **Combine the warm milk, melted butter, and sugar.** When the mixture is warm, but not hot to the touch, add the yeast, followed by the egg yolk and salt. Gradually work in the flour until you have a mixture that pulls away from the sides of the bowl. Turn out onto a lightly floured surface and knead for several minutes, until the dough bounces back when poked. Place in a greased bowl, cover, and let sit somewhere warm to rise until doubled in bulk, about an hour.

2. **Preheat the oven to 375°F** and line a baking sheet with parchment paper. Punch the dough down and break off pieces roughly the size of a golf ball. Press or roll each piece out into a flat circle about 5 inches across. Place a dollop of bean paste, about a tablespoon, in the center of the dough, then carefully fold the edges of the dough up and over, pinching to seal the paste in. Place each bun seam-side down on the prepared baking sheet, pressing gently on top to flatten them slightly. Repeat with all the dough, and press an indent into the middle of each bun. Using sharp scissors or a knife, make 5 slits radiating out from the center of each bun. Brush the buns with the remaining egg white and sprinkle a few sesame seeds around the indent of the bun. Cover and allow to rise for another 30 minutes.

3. **Once the buns have risen again, bake for 18 to 20 minutes** until the tops are golden brown and puffy. Remove from the oven and allow to cool before enjoying.

SOFT BANANA BREAD

SKILL LEVEL: Expert

PREP: 10 minutes

BAKING: 1 hour

MAKES: 1 loaf

PAIRS WELL WITH:
Breakfast of yogurt and granola; afternoon tea

The sweetest treat ever found in Scholomance, and just the thing to help you face whatever trials lie ahead. But pace yourself: Too much soft banana bread is known to be unkind to a necromancer's figure.

¼ cup unsalted butter, melted

⅓ cup granulated sugar

2 eggs

2 ripe bananas, mashed

½ cup buttermilk

2 cups flour

2 teaspoons baking powder

½ teaspoon baking soda

Pinch of salt

2 teaspoons diced candied ginger

FROSTING

4 ounces cream cheese, softened

¼ cup unsalted butter, softened

½ cup confectioners' sugar

1 tablespoon milk

Chopped walnuts, for garnish (optional)

1. **Preheat oven to 325°F.** Grease a 9 x 5 inch loaf pan with butter, then dust with flour. Set aside.

2. **In a medium bowl, cream together the butter and sugar.** Add the mashed bananas, eggs, and vanilla extract, stirring vigorously to mix. Add in the remaining ingredients and mix until you have a smooth batter. Empty into the prepared loaf pan and bake for about 50 to 60 minutes, until the top is a dark golden color. Remove from oven, let cool for 10 minutes, then turn out of the pan onto a cooling rack to cool the rest of the way.

3. **While the banana bread is baking, prepare the frosting:** Using a hand mixer on low, blend together the cream cheese and butter until light and fluffy, then add in the confectioners' sugar and milk. Set aside until banana bread is completely cool before spreading on top and sprinkling with nuts.

SWEET POTATO BREAD

SKILL LEVEL: Expert

PREP: 15 minutes

BAKING: About 2 hours

MAKES: 1 loaf

PAIRS WELL WITH: Chai tea, apple butter

Moist, dense, and richly flavored with an array of spices, this popular Northrend bread would be tasty on its own. But topped with caramel and crunchy nuts, it's absolutely decadent.

1 pound sweet potatoes (about 2 medium potatoes)

¼ cup whole milk

1 cup dark-brown sugar

2 large eggs

½ cup canola oil

1 teaspoon vanilla

1 teaspoon Holiday Spices (page 19)

½ teaspoon salt

1 teaspoon baking powder

½ teaspoon baking soda

1½ cups flour

Butter, for greasing pan

TOPPING

2 tablespoons salted butter

½ cup light brown sugar, packed

¼ cup heavy cream, warm

¼ teaspoon kosher salt

Dash of vanilla

Bourbon (optional)

¼ cup walnuts or pecans, roughly chopped

1. **Preheat the oven to 400°F.** Using a sharp knife, pierce the sweet potatoes several times, then place in the oven. Bake for about an hour, or until they are cooked through. Remove and allow to sit until they are cool enough to handle.

2. **Turn down the oven temperature to 325°F** and lightly butter a 9 x 5-inch loaf pan. Scoop the sweet potatoes out of their skins into a bowl and discard the skins. Add the milk and roughly mash the potatoes until there are no large pieces left. Add the sugar, eggs, oil, vanilla, and spices, beating to combine. Add the dry ingredients, scraping the sides of the bowl to make sure everything is incorporated.

3. **Pour the batter into the loaf pan,** and bake for about an hour, or until a toothpick poked into the middle comes out clean. Allow to cool for at least an hour, then run a butter knife along the sides of the pan and gently invert the pan to tip the bread out. Allow to cool on a wire rack until the bread is no longer warm to the touch. If you like, top with caramel and nuts, as below.

TOPPING: In a small saucepan over medium-high heat, whisk together butter, brown sugar, heavy cream, and salt. Bring to a boil (should take about 1 minute), then reduce heat. Simmer for 5 minutes, whisking frequently. Whisk in vanilla or bourbon if using, stir, then remove from heat and stir in the butter. Allow to cool for several minutes so the topping doesn't run off the bread. Spread the caramel over the cooled bread then sprinkle with the chopped nuts. Enjoy!

SOUPS AND STEWS

THE WAY OF THE BROTH

BEAN SOUP

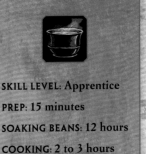

SKILL LEVEL: Apprentice

PREP: 15 minutes

SOAKING BEANS: 12 hours

COOKING: 2 to 3 hours

MAKES: 8 servings

PAIRS WELL WITH:
  Beer-Basted Boar Ribs
  (page 117)

A popular dish among the night elves of Kalimdor, this thick and hearty soup will sustain adventurers and innkeepers alike.

2 cups mixed dried beans (about 1 pound)

8 cups chicken broth

2 smoked ham hocks

1 teaspoon dried marjoram

2 tablespoons cumin

1 tablespoon olive oil

1 leek, white and pale-green parts chopped thin

2 cloves of garlic, minced

2 carrots, diced

1 celery rib, diced

Salt and pepper, to taste

1. **Place the beans in a large bowl and fill the bowl with water.** Soak for 8 to 12 hours, then pour off the remaining water.

2. **Place a large pot over medium heat.** Add the beans, chicken broth, ham hocks, marjoram, and cumin. Cook the soup, uncovered, for about 2 hours. If the beans are soft, move on to the next step, but if not, continue cooking for up to one more hour.

3. **In a medium frying pan, heat the olive oil over medium heat.** Add the leek and garlic, cooking until soft and fragrant, about 5 minutes. Add the carrots and celery along with a splash of water or broth (watch out for spattering oil), cover, and cook for another 10 minutes or so until the vegetables are soft. Stir into the beans and serve hot.

CLAM CHOWDER

SKILL LEVEL: Apprentice

PREP: 5 minutes

COOKING: 1 hour

MAKES: 4 servings

PAIRS WELL WITH: Rustic bread, spicy cured sausage, Versicolor Treat (page 191)

When it comes to a tasty clam chowder, it's hard to find one better than this classic dish that originated with the human fishermen of Westfall. The salt pork provides a richness that complements the classic seafood aroma and flavor, so the balance is just right.

¼ pound salt pork, diced small

2 medium-sized potatoes, peeled and chopped into bite-sized pieces

1 large shallot, chopped fine

1 teaspoon fresh or dried herbs, such as thyme, marjoram, etc.

Pinch of black pepper

One 10-ounce can baby clams

2 cups fish broth

Water to cover (2 to 4 cups)

1 cup milk

1 handful crushed water crackers or plain breadcrumbs

2 tablespoons butter

2 tablespoons flour

1. **Line the bottom of a large saucepan with the diced salt pork.** Now put a layer of potatoes on top of the salt pork, then a sprinkling of onion, herbs, and pepper, then a layer of clams. Pour the fish broth over, then add water to cover by about a half an inch.

2. **Bring the chowder to a simmer, cover, and cook for 30 minutes.** Then add the milk and crackers, and cook for another 10 minutes.

3. **In a separate pan, melt the butter.** Add the flour, and work together into a paste. Cook for a few minutes, then gradually add a ladle or two of the chowder broth, stirring quickly to combine into a thick soupy paste. Pour this back into the chowder pot, and cook for at least another 5 minutes to allow the chowder to thicken. Serve hot with extra crackers on the side.

DRAGONBREATH CHILI

SKILL LEVEL: Master

PREP: 15 minutes

COOKING: 2 hours

MAKES: 8 servings

PAIRS WELL WITH:
Cornmeal Biscuits
(page 69)

While this chili is unlikely to make you breathe flames, it lives up to its name in all other ways. Thick and flavorful, with just enough of a bite to satisfy, it's a hearty dish popular with melee types, who credit it with giving them a fighting edge before important battles. The original recipe comes from the swampland of Dustwallow Marsh in Kalimdor, but this version is a little different: No dragons were harmed in making it.

2 tablespoons vegetable oil

1 chili pepper, minced (jalapeño, or any others desired)

2 Thai peppers, minced

1 dried chipotle pepper, diced

½ onion, diced

1 pound ground beef

1 pound Italian sausage

1 pound chuck steak

2 teaspoons ground cumin

1 teaspoon

One 6-ounce can tomato paste

One 12-ounce bottle beer

2 cups beef broth

Two 15-ounce cans of chili beans

Two 28-ounce cans diced fire-roasted tomatoes

Grated cheddar cheese for topping

1. **Add the oil to a large stockpot over medium heat.** Add the peppers and the onion, then cook for about 5 minutes, or until brown and soft. Add the ground beef, sausage, and chuck steak, stirring until all the meat is browned, another 5 minutes or so.

2. **Add all the spices,** followed by the tomato paste, and stir so the paste and spices are evenly distributed. Pour in the beer and the beef broth, then add the beans and diced tomatoes. Lower the heat to a simmer and cook, uncovered, for about 2 hours, until the chili has thickened somewhat. Scoop into bowls and top with cheese.

COOK'S NOTES: This recipe is on the milder side of dragon-y, but I encourage you to amp up the spice level to your own preference! Also, choose a beer you like, but one that isn't too hoppy.

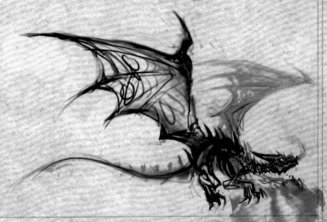

GOLDEN CARP CONSOMMÉ

SKILL LEVEL: Expert

PREP: 30 minutes

COOKING: 20 minutes

MAKES: 4 servings

PAIRS WELL WITH: White wine, a salad of crisp greens and fruit

Don't fret if you can't seem to hook that elusive golden carp—this recipe works just fine with any fish broth. Quick to make, this soup is flavorful and just the right amount of filling.

4 ounces matzo ball mix

32 ounces fish broth

2 shallots

½ cup chopped carrots

1 to 2 cloves garlic, chopped

Several slices fresh ginger

1 egg

Several threads of saffron

Scallions, for garnish

1. **Begin by making the matzo balls** according to the directions on their packaging.

2. **In a separate medium pot, combine the remaining ingredients except for the scallions.** Whisk for about a minute to break up the egg, then bring up to a low simmer and cook for about 20 minutes. Remove from heat and strain through cheesecloth into a clean bowl, keeping only the broth and discarding the rest. Add the cooked matzo balls, and serve warm.

LUKEWARM YAK ROAST BROTH

SKILL LEVEL: Expert

PREP: 5 minutes

COOKING: 2 to 3 hours

MAKES: 4 servings

PAIRS WELL WITH:
A Bloody Mary, spicy cured sausage

Contrary to its name, this dish is actually delightful when served hot. Previously enjoyed only by those who had climbed to Kun-Lai Summit, this flavorful, fortifying soup can now be made by anyone with the skill to combine these simple yet complementary ingredients.

2 cloves garlic, minced

1 leek, washed and chopped small

1 pound beef chuck roast

12 cups water

½ cup soy sauce

½ cup mushrooms

1 handful fettuccine pasta, broken in half

Salt and pepper, to taste

Dash of Sriracha sauce, to taste

Hard-boiled egg (optional)

1. **Combine all ingredients except the mushrooms and pasta in a large soup pot.** Bring to a boil, then reduce heat to a gentle simmer.

2. **Cook for 2 to 3 hours,** until the meat starts to fall apart. Remove from heat temporarily and shred the meat into bite-sized pieces with a pair of forks.

3. **Return to heat,** then add the mushrooms and reduce the heat to low.

4. **In a separate pot, boil salted water** and cook the pasta (if the pasta is cooked in the main pot, it will absorb too much of the broth) until the pasta is tender, about 5 to 10 minutes.

5. **Drain the pasta,** then add to the main pot. Ladle into bowls and serve. Top with a hard-boiled egg sliced in half (optional).

SPICED BLOSSOM SOUP

SKILL LEVEL: Apprentice

PREP: 5 minutes

COOKING: 20 minutes

MAKES: 4 servings

PAIRS WELL WITH:
Blue cheese, Mulgore
Spice Bread (page 83)

This restorative and fragrant soup is imbued with a multitude of floral flavors and spices. Found only in an ancient cache in the Vale of Eternal Blossoms, this delicious meal is sure to restore the body and mind of even the most exhausted warrior.

8 cups chicken broth

12 chamomile tea bags

1 bay leaf

1 teaspoon Ancient Pandaren Spices (page 17)

2 tablespoons sesame oil

1 to 2 cloves garlic, minced

1 to 2 shallots, sliced thin

1 tablespoon grated ginger

1 cup broccoli florets

½ small purple cabbage

Chamomile flowers, for garnish

1. **In a medium saucepan, bring the chicken broth to a simmer.** Add the tea bags and the bay leaf and allow to simmer for about 5 to 10 minutes. Pull the tea bags out, pressing any remaining liquid from them, and discard. Add the Ancient Pandaren Spices to the broth, and reduce heat to low while you prepare the vegetables.

2. **Heat the sesame oil in a frying pan over medium-low heat,** then add the garlic, shallots, and ginger. Cook for about 5 minutes, or until everything is soft and fragrant. Add the broccoli and cabbage, stirring to coat, then follow with a ladle of broth. Cover and allow to simmer until the vegetables are cooked through, about 5 minutes more. Remove from heat and pour everything into the pot with the broth. Serve immediately.

STEAMING CHICKEN SOUP

SKILL LEVEL: Master

PREP: 15 minutes

COOKING: About 2 hours

MAKES: 4 servings

PAIRS WELL WITH:
Conjured Mana Buns
(page 157), hot herbal tea

Sometimes, when the world outside is a frozen waste, a steaming bowl of chicken soup is just the thing to warm up a cold crusader. Brought to Icecrown by the Argent Crusade to fortify them in their campaign against the Lich King, this soup will ward off all manner of evils.

2 tablespoons salted butter

2 ribs celery, roughly chopped

1 large carrot, peeled and roughly chopped

2 cloves garlic, minced

1 tablespoon flour, for thickening

½ cup beer

8 cups chicken broth

1 teaspoon Northern Spices (page 20)

4 chicken drumsticks, uncooked

1 cup green peas

DUMPLINGS

2 cups flour

2 teaspoons baking powder

¾ teaspoon salt

2 tablespoons butter, melted and cooled

2 tablespoons fresh dill, stemmed and chopped small

¾ cup milk

1. **Melt the butter and oil in the bottom of a large soup pot over medium heat.** Add the celery, carrot, and garlic, cooking until they are soft, about 5 to 10 minutes. Sprinkle the flour over the vegetables, and stir to combine for several minutes until the flour starts to brown on the bottom of the pan. Pour in the beer, scraping up all the bits of the butter mixture, and simmer for 5 minutes. Increase the heat to medium-high, then add the broth, the Northern Spices, and the drumsticks. Cover and simmer for about an hour and a half, or until the meat has started to fall from the bones.

2. **While the soup is cooking, prepare the dumpling dough:** Combine the flour, baking powder, and salt in a medium bowl. Rub or cut in the butter, then the dill, tossing to distribute evenly. Gradually add milk until the mixture comes together in a wet mass. Cover until ready to make.

3. **Once the soup is done, move the drumsticks to bowls for serving, and keep warm.** Scoop out the dumpling dough in pieces roughly the size of golf balls. Drop the dumplings into the top of the still-simmering soup and cover the pot. Allow the dumplings to cook for about 10 minutes, then check one to see if the inside is cooked through. If not, flip all the dumplings and cook for another 5 minutes.

4. **To serve, scoop the dumplings into the bowls along with the drumsticks.** Ladle the soup over the top and enjoy.

COOK'S NOTE: If you are not a fan of dill, just about any other fresh herb will work, such as thyme or rosemary.

STEAMING GOAT NOODLES

SKILL LEVEL: Expert

PREP: About 30 minutes

COOKING: 15 minutes

MAKES: 4 servings

PAIRS WELL WITH: Fresh edamame, sparkling white wine

This flavorful Kun-Lai-style noodle soup is made from mutton and goat milk. As Brother Noodle says, "Steam goat noodle: Number one! Come fill belly with noodle, yes! Very good!"

6 to 7 ounces buckwheat soba noodles

2 tablespoons peanut oil

2 to 3 garlic cloves, minced

1 pound mutton or lamb, cut into bite-size pieces

1 tablespoon red curry paste

½ teaspoon turmeric

1 cup goat milk

⅓ cup peanut butter

2½ cups beef or chicken broth

1 teaspoon brown sugar

1 cup canned sliced bamboo shoots

Juice of ½ lime

Red pepper flakes, to taste

1 to 2 tablespoons parsley leaves, minced

3 to 4 green onions, sliced, for garnish

1. **Begin by cooking the noodles according to their directions,** draining and rinsing when they are just slightly underdone. Set aside.

2. **Heat the peanut oil over medium heat in a large frying pan with tall sides.** Add the garlic and fry until softened and fragrant, but not brown. Add the mutton and sear on all sides, about 3 to 4 minutes. Stir in the curry paste and turmeric, followed by the goat milk and peanut butter, and mix until smooth. Slowly pour in the broth, then add the brown sugar and bamboo shoots, and cook for another 5 to 10 minutes. Stir in the lime, red pepper, and parsley, then remove from heat.

3. **Divide the noodles between serving bowls, pour the sauce and mutton over the noodles,** then top with green onions and an extra shake of red pepper for garnish. Serve immediately.

WESTFALL STEW

SKILL LEVEL: Expert

PREP: 30 minutes

COOKING: About 3½ hours

MAKES: About 4 servings

PAIRS WELL WITH: A hunk of hearty bread, red wine, sharp cheeses

This nourishing stew has been made many different ways over the years. In lean times, with the people of Westfall under attack by bandits and gnoll raiders, murloc eyes and buzzard meat were commonly used. We wouldn't recommend it.

2 pounds quality stew beef, cut into bite-size pieces

Salt and pepper

½ cup diced bacon

2 tablespoons butter, divided

1 pound button mushrooms, sliced

1½ cups peeled pearl onions

1 tablespoon brown sugar

¼ cup flour

4 cups beef broth

2 cups red wine

1 teaspoon Northern Spices (page 20)

6 carrots, peeled and cut into bite-sized pieces

1 garlic head, cloves separated and peeled

1 cup pearled barley

2 bay leaves

1 tablespoon minced fresh parsley

1. **Preheat the oven to 475°F.** Toss the beef with the salt and allow to sit at room temperature for 30 minutes.

2. **Scatter the bacon in a 9 x 12-inch baking pan with tall sides,** along with 1 tablespoon butter, and cook for about 15 minutes, until the fat has rendered out. While the bacon is cooking, toss the mushrooms and pearl onions with the tablespoon of remaining butter and the brown sugar, and spread out on a baking sheet. Cook this for about 15 minutes until the liquid released by the mushrooms has mostly evaporated and the onions are slightly glazed. Remove to a bowl and set aside until the stew is nearly finished.

3. **Reduce oven temperature to 325°F.** Gradually add the flour to the hot pan with the bacon and bacon fat, whisking until there is no more flour visible. Gradually whisk in the broth, half the red wine, and the spices. Layer the carrots, garlic, barley, and bay leaves in the pan with the broth, then lay the stew meat over top of that. Pour in enough water to come most of the way up the meat, but not cover it. Cook for 1½ to 2 hours, then stir. Cook for another hour, stir, then add the remaining wine and the reserved onions and mushrooms. Cook for a final 30 minutes, then remove from oven. Discard the bay leaves, dish into serving bowls, and sprinkle with parsley.

WILDFOWL GINSENG SOUP

SKILL LEVEL: Master

PREP: 15 minutes

COOKING: 30 minutes

MAKES: 4 servings

PAIRS WELL WITH: Red Bean Buns (page 85)

This aromatic broth, rich with hearty noodles and topped with juicy duck meat, is lent a peppery bite by the ginger and chili. With just enough complexity to transcend rustic, this Valley of the Four Winds specialty is a warm and satisfying meal.

8 cups chicken broth

1-inch piece ginger, diced fine

2 to 3 whole star anise

2 tablespoons soy sauce

1 teaspoon salt

1 teaspoon red pepper flakes, or Thai peppers, to taste

3 tablespoons vegetable oil

2 whole duck breasts

2 cloves garlic, minced

Several handfuls baby spinach or baby bok choy, cut into thin slivers

One 10-ounce package dried egg noodles

1. **In a large saucepan, combine the chicken broth, ginger, anise, soy sauce, salt, and red pepper flakes.** Simmer this mixture for about 15 minutes, then remove the anise and turn down to low.

2. **Preheat the oven to 375°F.** Add the vegetable oil to an oven-safe skillet over medium heat. When the oil starts to shimmer, add the duck breasts, skin side down (be careful of oil spatters!). Sear the breasts for about 5 minutes, then flip the breasts and put the pan in the oven. Roast for another 8 to 10 minutes, then remove from the oven. Transfer to a cutting board and allow to sit until you are ready to serve.

3. **Return the skillet with the duck's cooking oil to a burner over medium low heat.** Add the garlic and cook until it is fragrant, but not brown. Turn off the heat and stir the baby spinach into the hot oil until it wilts. Set aside.

4. **In a large pot, bring water to a boil** and cook the noodles according to their instructions. When done, drain and toss with the garlic oil and greens to keep from sticking together. Add all of this to the broth.

5. **To serve, slice the duck breasts into bite-sized pieces.** Ladle the noodles and broth equally into four bowls, then top with the pieces of duck breast.

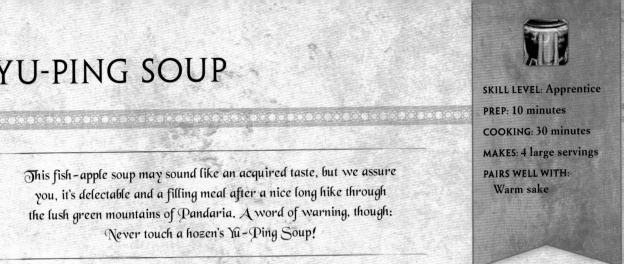

YU-PING SOUP

SKILL LEVEL: Apprentice

PREP: 10 minutes

COOKING: 30 minutes

MAKES: 4 large servings

PAIRS WELL WITH:
Warm sake

This fish-apple soup may sound like an acquired taste, but we assure you, it's delectable and a filling meal after a nice long hike through the lush green mountains of Pandaria. A word of warning, though: Never touch a hozen's Yu-Ping Soup!

8 cups chicken broth

1 cup apple cider

1 to 2 tablespoons apple cider vinegar

1 tablespoon freshly grated ginger

½ cup barley

1 clove garlic, minced

2 carrots, peeled and chopped

1 parsnip, peeled and chopped

About ½ cup cooked chicken meat (optional)

6 dried dates, halved

6 dried figs, halved

2 apples, peeled, cored, and cut into eighths

2 tablespoons goji berries

½ pound white fish, cut into small chunks

1 tablespoon Ancient Pandaren Spices (page 17)

1. **Combine the broth, cider, vinegar, ginger, barley, and vegetables in a medium pot.** Bring to a simmer and cook for about 20 minutes, or until the veggies have begun to soften. Add remaining ingredients, cook for another 10 minutes until the fish is cooked through, then remove from heat. Serve hot, straight away.

COOK'S NOTE: While this soup is still flavorful the next day, many of the ingredients will not hold their shapes, so it is best enjoyed the same day.

MAINS

THE WAY OF THE ENTRÉE

BEER-BASTED BOAR RIBS

SKILL LEVEL: Apprentice

PREP: 30 minutes

COOKING: 3 hours

MAKES: 4 servings, depending on appetite for ribs

PAIRS WELL WITH: Bean Soup (page 93), beer

The secret's in the malt! Ragnar Thunderbrew has been drawing patrons to his tavern for decades with the savory smell of his famous ribs. Now the old Thunderbrew family recipe for the best ribs in the Eastern Kingdoms is available to all.

One 3-pound rack of pork spareribs, or boar ribs, if available

Salt and pepper, to taste

1 tablespoon olive oil

2 shallots, diced

1 clove garlic, minced

2 teaspoons red curry paste

1 cup ketchup

1 bottle beer (Rhapsody Malt is best, but substitute in a pinch. The less hoppy, the better.)

2 tablespoons Worcestershire sauce

2 tablespoons molasses

1 tablespoon apple cider vinegar

1. **Preheat the oven to 275°F.** Line a rimmed baking sheet with aluminum foil and set a rack over top. Place the ribs on this rack, meaty side up, and sprinkle liberally with salt and pepper. Place in the oven to start slow-cooking.

2. **Place a saucepot over medium heat and add the oil, shallots, and garlic.** Cook until the shallots are soft and the garlic is fragrant, 3 to 5 minutes. Stir in the curry paste to coat the shallots and garlic, then add the remaining ingredients. Cook for 20 to 30 minutes, stirring occasionally, until the mixture has reduced to a semithick sauce. For a smoother sauce, blend the mixture with a submersible blender until no pieces of shallot or garlic remain.

3. **The ribs will slow cook for about 3 hours.** Baste with the sauce every 20 to 30 minutes or so (cover the underside a few times, too) until you've got a nice thick layer of tangy delicious sauce. Allow to cool slightly after cooking, and enjoy.

CRUNCHY SPIDER SURPRISE

SKILL LEVEL: Master

PREP: 5 minutes

FRYING: 30 minutes

MAKES: About 1 dozen balls

PAIRS WELL WITH: Hoisin dipping sauce, Wildfowl Ginseng Soup (page 111)

The surprise comes when, with a look of delighted satisfaction, happy customers ask you what it is. But, seriously, one should only use spider meat when there are absolutely no better options, so this recipe substitutes crab to get the same culinary crunch with less "eww" factor. Designed by a master chef tasked with feeding blood elf royalty on a budget, this recipe will surprise and delight those with even the most discerning palates.

1 egg, separated

About 8 ounces wonton wrappers

1 pound crabmeat, or imitation crab

1 teaspoon salt

1 teaspoon sugar

1 tablespoon cornstarch

Pinch each red and black peppers

Oil for frying

1. **In a small bowl, beat the egg white with a splash of water for a few seconds.** Set aside. Slice the wonton wrappers into very thin strips, and set those aside as well.

2. **Combine the crabmeat, salt, sugar, cornstarch, egg yolk, and seasoning in a food processor,** and blend until completely mixed. Bring about 2 inches of oil to medium heat in a small saucepan. Scoop out small portions of the crab mixture and form into balls roughly 2 inches across. Dip each ball into the beaten egg, then into the sliced wonton strips, taking care to cover the whole ball, and squeezing gently to secure the strips in place.

3. **Lower each wrapped ball into the hot oil,** and cook for several minutes on each side, until the wonton strips are crispy and the insides are cooked.

DIRGE'S KICKIN' CHIMAEROK CHOPS

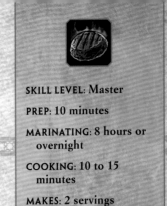

SKILL LEVEL: Master

PREP: 10 minutes

MARINATING: 8 hours or overnight

COOKING: 10 to 15 minutes

MAKES: 2 servings

PAIRS WELL WITH: Couscous or rice

Since it's no longer possible to get chimaerok tenderloins after the sinking of the Isle of Dread, we're making do with lamb chops. Do not, I repeat, do not disturb Prince Lakma, last of his kind. He's the one chimaerok left in Azeroth, and my friend simply cannot catch a break with all of you chasing after his legendary, savory haunches. Lamb chops are a fine substitute. Trust me.

1 tablespoon red curry paste

¼ cup rum or bourbon

½ cup chicken broth

1 pound lamb shoulder chops

SPICE RUB

1 teaspoon cumin

1 teaspoon paprika

1 teaspoon Aleppo pepper flakes, or other red pepper flakes

½ teaspoon each nutmeg and cinnamon

Pinch of salt

1 to 2 tablespoons olive oil

1. **Combine the red curry paste, rum, and chicken broth in an airtight bag or a shallow baking dish.** Place the lamb chops in this marinade, making sure to cover both sides of the meat, and let sit for at least 8 hours, or overnight.

2. **When you are ready to cook, combine the spices for the rub in a small bowl.** Place a large frying pan over medium heat and pour in the olive oil to begin heating it up. Meanwhile, pull the lamb chops out of the bag and set on a plate. Pat dry, then press half the spice mixture onto one side of the meat. Flip, and press the remaining spices onto the chops.

3. **Once the pan is hot, lower the chops in gently.** Cook on each side for about 4 to 5 minutes, until the lamb is cooked through to your preference. Remove from the pan and allow to rest for about 5 minutes under a tent of foil to keep it warm.

4. **If you like, you can make a small amount of sauce by pouring the rest of the marinade into the emptied pan,** and scraping to get up any spices that have cooked down. Stir for a few minutes, until the mixture has thickened somewhat, then strain into a small pitcher and serve alongside the chops.

FIRECRACKER SALMON

SKILL LEVEL: Apprentice

PREP: 1 hour

COOKING: 10 minutes

MAKES: 2 servings

PAIRS WELL WITH:
Wild Rice Cakes (page 61), sautéed green beans or asparagus

The warmth of the spices battles for dominance with the cool bite of the juniper, like the meeting of the cold glacial salmon and the fiery oven. Northrend food has never tasted so good.

Two 4-ounce salmon fillets

¼ cup sesame or vegetable oil

2 tablespoons soy sauce

2 tablespoons balsamic vinegar

2 teaspoons brown sugar

½ teaspoon Sriracha sauce

½ teaspoon Northern Spices (page 20)

½ teaspoon ground ginger

1. **Combine all the ingredients in a Ziploc bag,** and marinate the salmon in this mixture for at least an hour, or overnight in the fridge.

2. **While the salmon is marinating, line a small edged baking sheet with aluminum foil.** When you're ready to cook, turn the oven to a high broil, and place the salmon, skin side down, on the foil. Slide under the broiler and cook for 5 to 10 minutes, depending on the thickness of the fillets. When the fish flakes easily with a fork and is a pale pink color, it's done. Serve immediately.

FOREST STRIDER DRUMSTICKS

SKILL LEVEL: Apprentice

PREP: 10 minutes

COOKING: About 1 hour

MAKES: 4 legs

PAIRS WELL WITH: Root
beer float, Spicy
Vegetable Chips
(page 55)

These drumsticks . . . they're huge! There's nothing quite like Forest Strider Drumsticks to power you through a full round of the games and exotic delights offered at the Darkmoon Faire.

4 whole turkey legs, about 1 pound each

2 teaspoons coarse salt, smoked is best

1 teaspoon onion powder

1 teaspoon garlic powder

1 teaspoon ground coriander seed

1 teaspoon dried marjoram

½ teaspoon each paprika and black pepper

1. **Preheat the oven to 400°F** and line a baking sheet with foil. Rinse the turkey legs and pat them dry. Mix together all the dry ingredients for the rub. Apply the rub to each leg, pressing into the skin, and place legs on the prepared baking sheet.

2. **Bake at 400°F for 20 minutes,** then reduce the heat to 350°F and cook for another 30 minutes or so, until the skin is a dark brown and the internal temperature has reached 170°F.

GRACCU'S HOMEMADE MEAT PIE

SKILL LEVEL: Master

PREP: 1 hour

BAKING: 45 minutes

COOLING: 30 minutes

MAKES: 1 pie

PAIRS WELL WITH: Mashed potatoes, dark beer, Graccu's Mincemeat Fruitcake (page 173)

Smokywood Pastures brings all the best flavors of the holiday season to a market near you. Nothing will warm you to the bone during the Feast of Winter Veil like a slice of this delicious, meaty pie.

1 batch Flaky Pie Dough (page 22)

1 tablespoon butter, divided, plus more as needed

1 large leek, roughly chopped

3 cloves garlic, minced

2 carrots, peeled and chopped

2 sticks of celery, chopped

1 pound stew beef, cut into bite-sized pieces

½ pound sausage, cut into bite-sized pieces

1 pound ground beef or pork

3 tablespoons flour

½ teaspoon each minced fresh thyme and rosemary

½ teaspoon each salt and pepper

1 cup dark beer

1 cup beef stock

1 cup peas

1 egg, beaten with 1 teaspoon water, for glaze

1. **Make the Flaky Pie Dough ahead of time** and chill it while you prepare the pie filling.

2. **Heat half the butter in a large frying pan over medium heat.** Add in the leeks and garlic and cook for a few minutes until the leeks are just starting to soften. Add the carrots and celery next, cooking for another 5 minutes or so until the vegetables have begun to soften. Remove from heat and transfer to a separate pot large enough to hold all the pie filling.

3. **Melt the remaining butter in the same frying pan,** then add the stew beef. Turn the meat occasionally so it is browned on all sides, then scoop the beef to the same pot as the vegetables, leaving the butter and any fat in the pan. Cook the sausage, and likewise add to the pot. Finally, brown the ground meat in that same pan. When it is fully cooked, reduce heat to medium-low and drain off any excess fat, then sprinkle the meat with flour, stirring to coat. Pour in the beer and stir until the liquid thickens somewhat. Remove from heat and add to the other pot. Add all remaining ingredients except the peas and cook over medium-high heat for 30 to 40 minutes, until the liquid has reduced somewhat. Transfer to a large bowl and allow to cool completely.

Continued . . .

4. **Preheat oven to 375°F** and roll out the larger piece of pie dough to a roughly round shape. Drape this over your pie dish, letting the extra hang over the sides. Add the peas to the filling mixture, then carefully spoon the meats and vegetables into the pie shell, heaping them up in the middle and drizzling a little of the liquid over the top of everything. Cover with the other piece of rolled out dough, trim and crimp the edges, and use the trimmings to decorate, if you wish. Brush with beaten egg and bake for 45 minutes until the top crust is golden. Allow to cool at least 30 minutes before slicing.

COOK'S NOTE: The type of meats you use in this recipe is very adaptable, although the ratios should stay roughly the same: 1 pound cubed meat, 1 pound ground meat, and ½ pound sausage.

IRONFORGE RATIONS

SKILL LEVEL: Expert

PREP: 15 minutes

MAKES: 4 to 6 small servings

PAIRS WELL WITH: Beer, pickled vegetables, sharp cheese, mashed root vegetables

This dwarven recipe contains a beautiful pairing of haggis and beer, which has been the lunch of champions for over a thousand years. Simple, entirely satisfying, and perfect for when you need a quick meal on indefinite guard duty.

2 tablespoons butter

2 to 3 shallots, thinly sliced

Pinch of salt

One 15-ounce can of haggis

1 tablespoon flour

One 12-ounce beer

4 to 6 slices rustic bread, toasted

1 cup shredded cheddar cheese

Salt and pepper (optional)

1. **Melt the butter in a frying pan over medium heat.** Add the shallots and cook until they are soft and translucent. Add the salt and the haggis, breaking it up and spreading it around the pan until it is heated through. Work in the flour until it has been absorbed, then chase with about a third of the beer. The mixture should start forming into a sort of thick gravy. Depending on your preferences, add a little more of the beer for a looser texture.

2. **Divide the haggis evenly between your slices of bread,** top with cheddar cheese, and place under the broiler until the cheese has melted. Top with a pinch of salt and pepper to garnish, and enjoy!

OGRI'LA CHICKEN FINGERS

SKILL LEVEL: Apprentice

PREP: 10 minutes

BAKING: 15 to 20 minutes

MAKES: About 4 servings, or a dozen strips

PAIRS WELL WITH: Ketchup, honey, mustard, your choice of dipping sauce, French fries

If you've got a powerful hunger after venturing into the Blade's Edge Mountains, look no further for the cure than a nice basket of giant Ogri'la Chicken Fingers.

1 tablespoon olive oil

1½ cups panko breadcrumbs

1 teaspoon garlic powder

¼ cup Parmesan cheese

1 egg

1 tablespoon mustard

1 tablespoon flour

Pinch each salt and pepper

1 pound chicken breast, cut into 1-inch strips

1. **Preheat the oven to 400°F** and line a large baking sheet with parchment paper. Set a cooling rack atop this, which will help the chicken cook evenly.

2. **Heat the olive oil over medium heat in a wide skillet.** Pour in the breadcrumbs and the garlic powder, and stir occasionally as the breadcrumbs toast up to a golden brown color, about 5 minutes. Remove from heat and pour into a medium bowl. Once the breadcrumbs are cool, mix in the Parmesan cheese and set aside.

3. **In a separate bowl, mix together the egg, mustard, flour, salt, and pepper.** Working with one piece at a time, dip a strip of chicken into this batter, allowing the excess to drip off, then dip into the breadcrumbs, covering both sides. Place the breaded chicken on the rack, and repeat with the remaining pieces.

4. **Bake for about 15 to 20 minutes,** or until the chicken is done and the edges of the chicken strips have started to brown slightly. Serve immediately with your choice of dipping sauce.

ROASTED QUAIL

SKILL LEVEL: Expert

PREP: 10 minutes

COOKING: 25 minutes

MAKES: 2 servings

PAIRS WELL WITH:
Spiced pilaf

A much-loved meal around the south of the Eastern Kingdoms, these sweet and savory morsels are well worth the effort of making them. While ogres enjoy this dish as a light snack, polishing off a whole quail in a single crunchy bite, smaller races will find it's most easily eaten with one's hands.

6 quails

2 cloves fresh minced garlic

1 tablespoon fresh minced savory herbs (chef's choice), divided

1 large red onion, cut into eighths

2 tablespoons olive oil, divided

1 teaspoon balsamic vinegar

2 tablespoons brown sugar

Pinch of nutmeg

Salt and pepper, to taste

½ pound grapes, divided into small clusters

¼ cup apple cider

1. **Preheat the oven to 450°F.** Combine the minced garlic and the fresh herbs in a small bowl, then spread a little of the mixture inside each quail. Toss the onions with 1 tablespoon of the oil, balsamic vinegar, brown sugar, and nutmeg. Spread the onion mixture in the bottom of a roasting pan. Place the quail on top of the onions, breast side down. Cook for 10 minutes, then flip over. Brush with a little oil and sprinkle with salt and pepper.

2. **Spread the clusters of grapes around the quail,** pour the cider into the bottom of the pan, and return to the oven for another 10 to 15 minutes or so. If you'd like a more golden color, place the quail under the broiler for a few minutes until they are nicely browned.

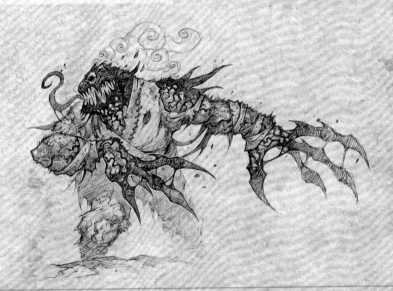

SAVORY DEVIATE DELIGHT

SKILL LEVEL: Master

PREP: 10 minutes

COOKING: 20 minutes

MAKES: 6 small tacos

PAIRS WELL WITH:
  Kungaloosh (page 204)

Somebody stole a recipe from a pirate named Stinkbraid, and strange things started happening to those who made the delicious dish. When you try Savory Deviate Delight, beware of flipping out. Or turning into a pirate.

Vegetable oil for frying

Tilapia fillets, cut in half

Salt and pepper

2 cups yellow corn

½ cup red bell pepper, diced

Splash white wine vinegar

6 small flour tortillas

½ cup tartar sauce

About 1 cup red cabbage, finely shredded

Pinch each salt and pepper

BATTER

1½ cups flour

¼ cup cornstarch

1½ cups buttermilk

Pinch each salt and cayenne pepper

1. **Pour about an inch of oil into a small frying pan** and begin heating over medium heat, to about 300°F. Combine all the ingredients for the batter in a small mixing bowl, whisking together until you have a thick, smooth mixture. Pat dry the fish fillets, and dip into the batter, then gently lower into the hot oil. Let strips of battered fish cook for a minute or two on each side until a nice golden color, then remove to a plate lined with paper towel to drain.

2. **In a separate pan, add a dash of oil,** then roast the corn and red pepper for a few minutes until they begin to brown, then add the splash of vinegar. Stir for another 30 seconds, and remove from heat.

3. **To put together the tacos, spread a dollop of tartar sauce down the middle of a tortilla.** Lay one piece of fried fish over that, then top with the corn mixture and cabbage. Serve immediately.

SKEWERED PEANUT CHICKEN

SKILL LEVEL: Expert

PREP: 5 to 10 minutes

MARINATING: At least 4 hours

COOKING: 10 minutes

MAKES: 4 servings

PAIRS WELL WITH: Rice, sautéed vegetables

This pandaren specialty features tender, flavorful chicken, doused in a rich, creamy peanut sauce. Served over a bed of rice, and garnished with fresh tomatoes and snap peas, who could want more?

4 large chicken breasts

MARINADE

½ cup soy sauce

1 teaspoon freshly grated ginger

Pinch of salt

Cherry tomatoes and snap peas, for garnish (optional)

SAUCE

¼ cup creamy peanut butter

One 13-ounce can coconut milk

¼ cup brown sugar

1 tablespoon soy sauce

1½ tablespoons red curry paste

1. **Combine the marinade ingredients along with the chicken breasts in a large bowl** or a sturdy plastic bag. Refrigerate for at least 4 hours, or overnight, stirring occasionally to make sure the meat is completely covered. Soak four wooden skewers in water.

2. **Make the sauce by combining the sauce ingredients in a small saucepan over medium heat.** Gently stir everything together until the mixture is creamy and smooth. Remove from heat and allow to cool slightly.

3. **Thread the whole chicken breasts onto the wooden skewers.** Grill over medium-high heat, flipping halfway through, until the meat is cooked through, about 10 minutes. Plate the chicken, drizzle with sauce, and enjoy!

COOK'S NOTE: You may garnish the skewers with cherry tomatoes and snap peas, if you like, but do so after grilling; the vegetables will likely overcook otherwise.

SLOW-ROASTED TURKEY

SKILL LEVEL: Expert

PREP: 10 minutes

COOKING: 20 minutes per pound

MAKES: 1 roasted turkey, for many, many servings

PAIRS WELL WITH: Candied Sweet Potatoes (page 31), Cranberry Chutney (page 35), Hot Apple Cider (page 202)

What better way to give thanks for a bountiful harvest than with this showpiece of Pilgrim's Bounty? This tender and flavorful bird will satisfy everyone in your party, but don't be surprised if it also lures a few strangers who are eager for a serving!

1 whole turkey, 12 pounds or more

2 cups chicken broth

2 cups apple cider

1 tablespoon honey

1 onion, roughly chopped

1 batch Spice Bread Stuffing (page 51), optional

¼ cup butter, melted

¾ cup white wine

1 tablespoon Autumnal Herbs (page 18)

Salt, to taste

Cornstarch, for gravy

1. **Preheat the oven to 425°F** and place a rack into a large roasting pan with tall sides. Pour the chicken broth, apple cider, and honey into the bottom of the pan, and add the chopped onion. Stuff the turkey (if using stuffing) and place on the rack.

2. **Combine the melted butter, wine, and Autumnal Herbs in a small bowl.** Brush this mixture over the turkey, then sprinkle with the salt to help the browning process.

3. **Cook the turkey for 30 minutes** then reduce the heat to 350°F. Baste the turkey with the juices in the pan every 45 minutes or so for flavor and color. The turkey should cook for about 20 minutes per pound, until the internal temperature has reached 165°F. If the bird starts to brown too much, place a loose tent of tin foil over top, making sure it doesn't actually touch the skin. You can also add a cup at a time of extra water to the bottom of the pan if too much has cooked off.

4. **When done, remove the turkey from the oven,** transfer to a platter, and make the gravy.

GRAVY: For the best gravy, let the drippings from the pan sit for a brief time to allow the fat to rise to the top, where you can strain or skim it off and discard. Pour the drippings into a wide pan over low heat.

5. **Mix the cornstarch with a splash of water to dissolve it,** then whisk it into the drippings. Use about 1 teaspoon cornstarch for every cup of drippings, or more if you prefer a thicker gravy.

TENDER SHOVELTUSK STEAK

SKILL LEVEL: Apprentice

PREP: 5 minutes

COOKING: 15 minutes

SAUCE: 10 minutes

MAKES: 2 servings

PAIRS WELL WITH: Roasted
green vegetables,
Sautéed Carrots (page
45), rich red wine

Think of a cross between a boar and a stag, and you've got yourself a shoveltusk. This steak is beloved by magic users, who claim it gives them just a little bit of an edge in casting their spells. Don't ask us how.

2 steaks, about 1 pound each, at room temperature

1 tablespoon olive oil

1 to 2 tablespoons unsalted butter

1 tablespoon salt

1 teaspoon Northern Spices (page 20)

1 clove garlic, minced

1 cup red wine

1. **Melt the olive oil and butter in a skillet over medium-high heat.** Mix together the salt, Northern Spices, and garlic in a small bowl, then liberally cover both sides of the steaks with the seasoning.

2. **Lower the steaks into the pan and sear for a minute or two.** Flip and cook for another minute or two, then carefully add the wine—the pan will hiss and spatter for a moment. Cook for a few more minutes for medium-rare steaks. When the meat is done to your liking, remove to a cutting board, cover loosely with foil, and allow the steaks to rest while you finish the sauce. Reduce the liquid in the pan until it has thickened somewhat but is still pourable, roughly 10 minutes.

WINTER VEIL ROAST

SKILL LEVEL: Expert

PREP: 15 minutes

COOKING: 1 hour

MAKES: 4 to 6 servings

PAIRS WELL WITH:
  Sautéed Carrots (page 45), mashed potatoes, red wine

The rich sauce is imbued with the familiar smells and flavors of the merry Winter Veil season, which will remind you of holidays past whenever you enjoy this dish.

ROAST

1 top-round roast, about 3 pounds

Olive oil

Salt and pepper

SAUCE

1½ cups red wine

3 shallots, roughly chopped

1-inch knob ginger, diced

A pinch of ground cinnamon

A pinch of freshly ground black pepper

1 teaspoon balsamic vinegar

4 tablespoons salted butter

1. **Preheat the oven to 400°F.** Rub the roast all over with the oil, then sprinkle liberally with salt and pepper. Place in a roasting tray and cook for about an hour, or until the temperature of the middle of the roast registers about 145°F for medium doneness.

2. **While the roast is cooking, prepare the sauce.** Bring all the ingredients except the butter to a simmer in a small saucepan, then gently reduce the mixture for about 10 to 15 minutes. Taste and adjust the seasonings accordingly, then whisk in the butter a little bit at a time until the sauce looks smooth. Strain out the shallots and ginger, then spoon over the slices of roast.

DESSERTS

THE WAY OF THE SWEET

BLOODBERRY TART

SKILL LEVEL: Expert

PREP: 15 minutes

BAKING: 45 minutes

COOLING: 2 hours

MAKES: 8 servings

PAIRS WELL WITH:
A splash of heavy cream, herbal tea

It's a mystery why nobody but alchemists go to Quel'Danas to pick bloodberries—they're delicious! While this recipe doesn't provide the same beneficial properties as the bloodberry version, it gives a fair approximation of the bloodberry's color and flavor.

1 batch Flaky Pie Dough (page 22)

1 pound crushed raspberries

1 pound blueberries

2 cups sugar

3 tablespoons pectin

2 tablespoons balsamic vinegar

Pinch of ground cardamom

1. **Begin by making the crust:** Roll out the batch of Flaky Pie Dough into a large circle about ⅛-inch thick. Carefully drape this dough over a 9-inch tart pan or a standard pie pan. Press the dough into the bottom of the pan, and then trim off any excess. If using a pie pan, you may wish to pinch the crust into a decorative shape. Use the extra dough to add cut-out embellishments. Place the prepared shell in the freezer for the 15 minutes or so it will take to make the filling.

2. **Preheat the oven to 375°F.**

3. **Place the raspberries in a small saucepan over medium-low heat,** and cook gently until the berries fall apart. Strain the berry pulp into a clean medium bowl, discarding the seeds. Return to the pan, and add the remaining ingredients. Bring to a boil and cook for a few minutes. Remove from heat and pour into the bowl. Place the berry mixture in the fridge to cool.

4. **When you are ready to make the tart, preheat the oven to 375°F.** Pour the berry filling into the crust, then slide the baking sheet into the oven. Bake for about 45 minutes, or until the crust is golden and the filling is bubbling.

5. **Carefully remove the tart from the oven,** still on the baking sheet, and allow to cool completely, for about 2 hours, before cutting, otherwise the filling will be runny.

CHEERY CHERRY PIE

SKILL LEVEL: Master

PREP: 15 minutes

BAKING: 40 minutes

MAKES: 1 pie, or about 8 servings

PAIRS WELL WITH: Fruity red wine or port

This pie is dark, but so is Gilneas, and nobody knows how to make a pie like Chris Moller. The rich flavors of this recipe are decadent and warming—just the thing to keep you off dangerous streets at night.

1 batch Flaky Pie Dough (page 22)

20 ounces of frozen sweet dark cherries, thawed

1 cup cherry juice

¾ cup sugar

3 tablespoons cornstarch

2 teaspoons cinnamon

½ teaspoon ground cardamom

½ teaspoon ground ginger

1 egg, beaten with 1 teaspoon water, for egg wash

1. **Preheat the oven to 400°F.** Roll out half of the pie dough, and gently drape over a pie pan. Trim off any excess dough and set aside.

2. **Strain the cherries, reserving any extra juice;** if you don't get much juice from them, or if you are using fresh cherries, you may need to supplement with a little extra juice. In a medium bowl, mix together the sugar, cornstarch, and spices, then add the cherries and juice. Stir to make sure it is all evenly mixed, then pour into the prepared pie shell.

3. **Roll out the other half of the dough and cut into strips for the lattice top crust.** Working with one strip at a time, weave the lattice together. You can decorate the edge of the crust with any remaining dough scraps. Brush with the beaten egg, taking care not to spread too much of the filling onto the crust.

4. **Bake the pie for about 40 minutes until the crust is a rich golden color.** Allow to cool for at least 2 hours before slicing, to give the filling time to set.

COOK'S NOTE: For an extra treat, replace half the cherry juice with red wine or port, which will give the pie an even more pronounced mulled-wine flavor, perfect for winter.

CHOCOLATE CELEBRATION CAKE

SKILL LEVEL: Master

PREP: 20 minutes

BAKING: 25 minutes

ASSEMBLY: 10 minutes

MAKES: 1 cake, at least 8 servings

PAIRS WELL WITH: Vanilla or ginger ice cream, a peppery red wine, Deep-Fried Plantains (page 163)

There's surely no better way to mark a special occasion than with a cake like this one. Each bite bursts with warming spices, while the smooth nuttiness of the whipped cream manages to keep it feeling light. So go ahead, have another slice. You're celebrating!

1 batch of Whipped Cream (page 21)

1½ cups flour

1 cup sugar

½ cup cocoa powder

1 teaspoon baking soda

½ teaspoon salt

1 teaspoon ground cinnamon

½ teaspoon ground ginger

¼ teaspoon cayenne pepper

1 cup buttermilk

½ cup vegetable oil

2 teaspoons vanilla

CANDIED NUTS

½ cup sugar

2 tablespoons water

½ cup hazelnuts, toasted

Pinch of salt

1. **Preheat oven to 350°F.** Grease and flour two 8-inch round baking pans.

2. **Sift together the dry ingredients,** then add the remaining ingredients and beat together with a mixer for a minute or two, until you have a nice, smooth, light batter. Divide evenly between the two baking pans.

3. **Bake for 20 to 25 minutes,** until a toothpick comes out clean. Cool for 5 minutes, then transfer to a cooling rack. Allow to cool completely before assembling.

4. **To assemble, set one cake layer on a serving platter.** Spread about a third of the whipped cream over the top of the layer, then gently lower the second layer on top of that. Repeat the process with another third of the whipped cream, then put the rest into a piping bag with a star tip. Pipe decorative clusters of whipped cream along the bottom of the cake and over the top. Dot the top of the cake with some candied hazelnuts (recipe below) and serve immediately.

CANDIED NUTS: Line a baking sheet with a silicone mat or parchment paper and set aside. In a small saucepan over medium heat, cook the sugar and water until the sugar has dissolved. Turn up the heat to a gentle simmer and cook for a few minutes, until the color has darkened to a rich amber. Remove from heat, stir in the nuts and salt, and swirl to make sure all the nuts are covered.

5. **Working quickly but carefully, tilt the pan and pull the nuts out to fall onto the prepared baking sheet.** Separate the nuts to keep them from clumping together. You can also pour the whole mixture out onto the pan and separate the nuts away from the sugar with a fork. Immediately soak the pan with warm water to dissolve the remaining sugar. Allow to cool, then decorate the cake with the candied nuts.

CHOCOLATE COOKIES

SKILL LEVEL: Apprentice

PREP: 30 minutes

CHILLING: 1 hour

BAKING: About 10 minutes

MAKES: About 2 dozen cookies

PAIRS WELL WITH: Ice cold milk, hot cocoa, ice cream

There's nothing like a cookie to make you feel a little better when you're down. With their dark chocolaty zip and peppery punch, these crispy morsels will help you get through even the worst cataclysms.

1 stick unsalted butter, room temperature

½ cup granulated sugar

1 egg

1 teaspoon vanilla

½ teaspoon salt

½ cup unsweetened cocoa powder

1 teaspoon ground cinnamon

Pinch of cayenne pepper

1¼ to 1½ cups flour

1 batch Royal Icing for Cookies (page 21)

1. **In a medium bowl, cream together the butter, sugar, egg, and vanilla until you have a nice smooth mixture.** Add in the salt and spices, incorporating each completely. Gradually add the flour until you have a dough that is no longer sticky. Form into a disc, wrap in plastic, and chill for at least an hour.

2. **When ready, preheat the oven to 375°F** and line a baking sheet with parchment. Roll your dough out on a lightly floured surface to about ¼-inch thick. Cut into desired shapes and place on prepared baking sheet. Bake for about 10 minutes, then remove to wire racks to cool completely before icing.

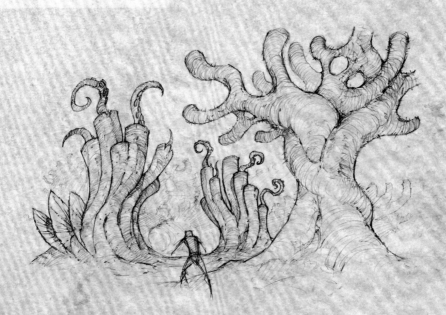

CONJURED MANA BUNS

SKILL LEVEL: Expert

PREP: 15 minutes

RISING: 1½ hours

BAKING: 15 to 20 minutes

MAKES: About 24 buns

PAIRS WELL WITH: Hot Apple Cider (page 202)

You don't have to be a sorcerer to whip up a batch of these nutty, soft morsels. Neither the glaze nor the filling is overly sweet, which means you can sneak at least one extra to power you through your next adventure.

DOUGH

¾ cup milk, warm

½ cup brown sugar

1 tablespoon instant yeast

½ cup butter, melted

1 egg

½ teaspoon salt

4½ cups flour

FILLING

4 tablespoons butter, softened

2 teaspoons flour

2 tablespoons brown sugar

2 tablespoons cinnamon

½ cup walnuts, finely chopped, plus more for sprinkling if needed

BROWN SUGAR GLAZE

1 cup brown sugar

1 tablespoon butter

1 tablespoon flour

½ cup heavy cream, plus more as needed

Dash of vanilla

1. **In a large bowl, combine the warm milk and the sugar,** stirring until the sugar dissolves. Add the yeast, followed by the butter and the egg, stirring to combine. Add in the salt, followed by the flour, gradually, until you have a workable dough. Turn out onto a lightly floured surface and knead until the dough bounces back when poked, under 5 minutes. Place in a lightly greased bowl, cover, and allow to rise in a warm spot until doubled in size, about an hour. Prep the filling by creaming the dry ingredients with the butter; set aside.

2. **Butter four muffin tins and set aside** (or two tins, and work in stages). When the dough has risen, roll it out on a lightly floured surface to a large rectangle, roughly 24" x 12". Spread the filling evenly over the surface, leaving only a small strip along one long edge uncovered. Starting on the opposite long edge, begin rolling the dough into a tight tube. Using a sharp knife, slice the roll every 1 inch, then place one bun in each muffin space in the prepared tins. Cover and allow to rise again for about 20 minutes.

3. **Preheat the oven to 350°F** and bake the buns for 15 to 20 minutes, until the tops are golden brown. While they are baking, make the glaze: Melt the brown sugar in a small saucepan over medium-low heat, then stir in the flour until you have no dry lumps. Pour the milk in, and when you have a smooth consistency, remove from heat and add the butter and vanilla.

4. **When the buns are done, remove them from the oven,** and while the buns are still warm, move them from the pans to a cooling rack. Spoon the glaze over the top of each bun. Sprinkle with extra nuts, if you like, and enjoy.

CONJURED MANA STRUDEL

SKILL LEVEL: Master

PREP: 20 minutes

RISING: 1 hour

BAKING: 20 minutes

MAKES: 1 strudel

PAIRS WELL WITH: Finger sandwiches, light luncheon of meats and cheeses, mimosas

Not just any mage can conjure up this mana strudel—but with some dedication and time spent on mastering your magical skills, this delicious high-level treat can be yours.

½ batch Buttery Pastry Dough (page 23)

½ cup cherry or red berry jam

4 ounces cream cheese

2 tablespoons granulated sugar

¼ teaspoon vanilla

Egg to glaze

1 batch Drizzled Icing and Glaze (page 22)

Fresh berries, for garnish (optional)

1. **Preheat the oven to 400°F** and set aside a large baking sheet.

2. **In a small bowl, mix together the cream cheese, sugar, and vanilla** until smooth.

3. **Roll out the dough on top of a piece of lightly floured parchment paper** into a square roughly 14 x 14 inches, and no thicker than ¼ inch. Carefully spread the cream cheese mixture in a strip down the middle third of the square, covering roughly ⅓ of the dough and leaving an inch and a half bare on either end. Spread the jam over the cream cheese mixture.

4. **Using a sharp knife, cut out the corners of the dough,** leaving a little flap at both ends of the filling. Slice the sides of the strudel into 1-inch wide strips. Trim the sides, if necessary, for a straighter line. Fold both the end flaps up over the filling, then starting on one end, begin laying the strips diagonally over the filling toward the other side. Alternate sides, always laying the new strip over the previous one. Continue until the whole pastry is bundled up. Taking great care, pick up the parchment paper and slide it onto the baking sheet. Beat egg and brush onto the strudel.

5. **Cover lightly and allow to rise for about 20 minutes,** then uncover and place in the oven. Bake at 400°F for about 20 minutes, or until the top of the strudel is a nice warm golden color. Remove from oven and allow to cool completely before icing. Garnish with fresh berries, if you like.

DALARAN BROWNIE

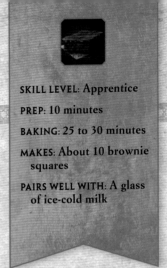

SKILL LEVEL: Apprentice

PREP: 10 minutes

BAKING: 25 to 30 minutes

MAKES: About 10 brownie squares

PAIRS WELL WITH: A glass of ice-cold milk

Make sure you're seated while you enjoy this delicious baked good; it will take all your concentration to navigate each gooey, decadent bite. Oozing with a chocolate glaze and dusted with cocoa and spice, these are the brownies to beat all brownies. But don't set a bad example—bring enough to share!

½ cup butter

⅓ cup unsweetened cocoa powder

¾ cup granulated sugar

2 eggs

1 teaspoon vanilla

½ cup all-purpose flour

¼ teaspoon salt

¼ teaspoon baking powder

GLAZE

3 tablespoons butter

⅓ cup unsweetened cocoa powder

2 tablespoons milk

1 cup confectioners' sugar

1 tablespoon each cocoa powder and ground cinnamon, for dusting

1. **Preheat the oven to 350°F,** and grease an 8 x 8-inch pan.

2. **In a medium saucepan, melt the butter and cocoa powder.** Remove from heat and stir in the sugar, eggs, and vanilla until you have a smooth mixture. Add the dry ingredients, stirring vigorously to combine. Pour the mixture into the prepared pan and smooth the top.

3. **Bake for 25 to 30 minutes, then remove from the oven to cool.** Prepare the glaze: Melt the butter in a small saucepan over medium-low heat, then add the cocoa powder and milk, stirring to combine. Gradually add the confectioners' sugar, stirring vigorously until you have a smooth, thick-but-pourable consistency.

4. **Slice the cooled brownies into squares,** then spoon the glaze over the tops, allowing it to run over the sides, if you like. Dust the tops of the brownies with the cocoa and cinnamon.

DEEP-FRIED PLANTAINS

SKILL LEVEL: Expert

PREP: 10 minutes

COOKING: About 5 minutes

MAKES: 2 small servings or enough topping for 4 desserts

PAIRS WELL WITH: Chocolate Celebration Cake (page 153), vanilla ice cream, yogurt, oatmeal

This sweet treat is Tyrande Whisperwind's guilty pleasure. Fried to the point of just shy of too soft, this recipe brings out the best flavors of all its ingredients.

Olive oil

1 underripened banana, sliced ½-inch thick

1 tablespoon honey

1 tablespoon hot water

Pinch of cinnamon

Sesame seeds for topping (optional)

1. **Add just a dash of oil to a pan over medium-low heat.** When the oil is hot, add the banana slices and cook for a couple of minutes on each side. While they cook, combine the honey, cinnamon, and hot water in a small bowl. When the fruit slices are golden on each side, remove from heat and pour in the honey mixture. Allow to cool for a minute or so before enjoying.

DELICIOUS CHOCOLATE CAKE

SKILL LEVEL: Master

PREP: 20 minutes

FROSTING: 4 hours to chill

BAKING: 30 minutes

MAKES: 1 cake, at least 8
large servings

PAIRS WELL WITH:
Fresh raspberries,
sparkling wine

Although it's a bit tricky to make, there are few desserts as famous throughout Azeroth as this Delicious Chocolate Cake. With a dash of rose water to replace the impossible-to-find mageroyal, and fortified with a splash of port, this recipe is like fireworks of flavor for your mouth.

½ cup hot water

4 ounces white baking chocolate, chopped

1 cup butter, softened

1½ cups white sugar

3 eggs

2 teaspoons vanilla

1 cup buttermilk

2½ cups all-purpose flour

1 teaspoon baking soda

½ teaspoon baking powder

½ teaspoon salt

Starfruit and fresh raspberries, for garnish

1. **Begin by making the frosting, which needs to chill for four hours.** Break up the chocolate into a medium bowl. Heat half of the cream in a small saucepan until just starting to steam, but not yet simmering. Remove from heat and pour over the chocolate. Stir until the chocolate has completely melted into the cream. Cover and chill for at least 4 hours.

2. **Preheat the oven to 350°F,** and prep two 8-inch-round cake pans by greasing them and lining the bottom with a disc of parchment paper.

3. **In a small saucepan, melt the white chocolate in the hot water** until you have a smooth consistency. Set aside to cool, and in a large bowl, cream together the butter and sugar. Mix in the eggs and vanilla, then alternate the dry ingredients with the buttermilk. Finally, fold in the melted white chocolate.

4. **Pour the batter into the prepared pans and bake for about 30 minutes,** or until a toothpick inserted in the middle of the cake comes out clean. Allow the cake layers to cool in the pans for about 10 minutes, then gently tip out onto a cooling rack. Leave the layers to cool completely while you finish preparing the frosting and filling.

Continued . . .

DELICIOUS CHOCOLATE CAKE (CONTINUED)

FILLING

1 cup raspberries, fresh or frozen

¼ cup sugar

½ teaspoon rose water

1 tablespoon port

¼ cup Whipped Cream Frosting (see below)

FROSTING

8 ounces white baking chocolate

2 cups whipping cream, divided

Green food coloring (optional)

5. **After chilling the white chocolate and cream mixture, whip it with an electric mixer for several minutes until it is fluffy.** In a separate bowl, whip the other cup of cream until it forms soft peaks. Fold this into the white chocolate mixture, then beat again for a couple of minutes until it holds its shape. Take care not to over-mix! Set aside the ¼ cup needed for the filling, then divide the remainder in half. Into one half, gently mix the green food coloring, if using, until you get a shade you like. Leave the other half white.

6. **Combine all the ingredients for the filling except the frosting in a small bowl,** mashing the berries until you have a somewhat thick paste. Gently fold in the reserved frosting until you have a nice pink mixture.

7. **When the filling, frosting, and cake layers are all made and cooled, it's time to assemble the cake.** Begin by placing one cake layer on your serving plate. Place about two thirds of the white frosting onto the single layer, and gently spread a thin coating along the top, then work the frosting down onto the sides, covering the cake. Spread the filling on top of that, then the second cake layer. Carefully spread the remaining white frosting onto the sides of the top layer. Top the cake with the green frosting, and garnish with raspberries and sliced starfruit.

GINGERBREAD COOKIES

SKILL LEVEL: Apprentice

PREP: 20 minutes

BAKING: 10 minutes

MAKES: About 2 dozen

PAIRS WELL WITH: Winter
Veil Eggnog (page 210)

There's no recipe more beloved by Greatfather Winter than these scrumptious Gingerbread Cookies. If you don't have time to visit him in person or don't want to face the crowds, leave a plate out overnight with a glass of ice-cold milk.

½ cup unsalted butter

¾ cup dark brown sugar

1 egg

1 teaspoon freshly grated ginger

2 teaspoons Holiday Spices (page 19)

1 teaspoon vanilla

¼ cup molasses

2 cups all-purpose flour

½ teaspoon baking soda

Pinch of salt

1 batch Royal Icing for Cookies (page 21)

1. **In a medium bowl, cream together the butter and sugar until smooth.** Add the egg, followed by the spices and vanilla. Finally, add the molasses, then the dry ingredients, mixing until it comes together in a nice cohesive dough. Chill for at least an hour.

2. **When you are ready to make the cookies, preheat oven to 350°F** and line a baking sheet with parchment paper. Roll the dough out to about ¼-inch thickness, cut into desired shapes, and place on the baking sheet. Bake for about 10 minutes, then cool completely on racks before icing.

GOBLIN SHORTBREAD

SKILL LEVEL: Apprentice

PREP: 5 minutes

BAKING: About 15 minutes

MAKES: 10 pieces

PAIRS WELL WITH:
Afternoon tea

The goblins of the Bilgewater Cartel once thrived on the Isle of Kezan. Although the goblins were forced to flee, this recipe made the journey with them to Kalimdor. They've added some more tropical ingredients since then, but these simple shortbread cookies will always remind goblins of their old home.

½ cup salted butter, room temperature

½ cup sugar

Pinch nutmeg

1 teaspoon lime zest

¼ cup pistachios, roughly chopped

1¼ cups all-purpose flour

1. **Preheat the oven to 350°F,** and set out a baking sheet lined with parchment paper.

2. **In a medium bowl, cream together the butter, sugar, nutmeg, and lime zest.** Add the pistachios and flour, and continue to work until the mixture comes together into a good dough.

3. **Turn the dough out onto the prepared baking sheet,** then pat into a smooth disc about 9 inches across. Using a sharp knife, make 5 cuts across the dough to form 10 wedges, then prick the tops of each with the tines of a fork.

4. **Bake until the edges of the shortbread are just starting to brown,** about 15 minutes.

GRACCU'S MINCEMEAT FRUITCAKE

SKILL LEVEL: Master

PREP: 15 minutes

BAKING: 1 hour, 15 minutes

COOLING, DECORATION: 45 minutes

MAKES: 1 fruitcake

PAIRS WELL WITH: Winter Veil Eggnog (page 210)

No treat that makes the rounds during the Feast of Winter Veil is quite so anticipated as Master Chef Graccu's delicious fruitcake. Although this dessert is made with simple dried fruits, the spices from the mincemeat ramp up the flavor of the whole, while the brandy icing gives a nod to the traditional holiday treatment.

1 stick butter (½ cup)

⅔ cup sugar

Zest of 1 orange (about 1 tablespoon)

2 eggs

¾ cup buttermilk

One 27-ounce jar of mincemeat (or one 8-ounce box)

½ teaspoon baking soda

2 teaspoons baking powder

½ teaspoon salt

3 cups flour

1 cup dried currants

¾ cup diced candied ginger

BRANDY ICING

1 cup confectioners' sugar, sifted

1 tablespoon orange zest

Dash of vanilla

1 to 2 tablespoons brandy

About 10 maraschino cherries, halved, for garnish (optional)

1. **Preheat the oven to 350°F,** and lightly grease a Bundt pan.

2. **In a large bowl, beat together the butter, sugar, and zest until light and fluffy.** Add the eggs one at a time, continuing to blend until fully incorporated. Add the buttermilk, followed by the mincemeat, baking soda, baking powder, and salt. Gradually add the flour 1 cup at a time, mixing well. When the batter is smooth, fold in the currants and candied ginger, making sure they are evenly distributed throughout the mixture.

3. **Pour the batter into the greased pan and bake for an hour.** Check to see if it is done by piercing with a toothpick; if the toothpick comes out clean, the cake is done. If not, return to oven and continue to bake for another 10 minutes, then check again. Repeat this until the cake is done. Allow the cake to cool for 10 minutes in the pan, then gently tip out onto a cooling rack. Let sit for another 30 minutes, or until it is cool to the touch, otherwise the icing will run off.

4. **In a small bowl, combine confectioners' sugar, zest, vanilla, and brandy.** Add enough milk to make a thick, pourable consistency. Carefully spoon over cake and garnish with maraschino cherries.

MANGO ICE

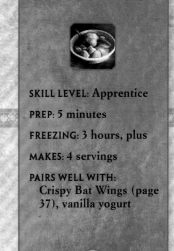

SKILL LEVEL: Apprentice

PREP: 5 minutes

FREEZING: 3 hours, plus

MAKES: 4 servings

PAIRS WELL WITH:
   Crispy Bat Wings (page
   37), vanilla yogurt

This light, fruity, and refreshing dessert is thought to have been a favorite among the ancient mogu of Pandaria. Now that you don't have to travel all the way to the Vale of Eternal Blossoms to obtain the ingredients, you can enjoy this treat at home.

1 cup milk

2 tablespoons sweetened condensed milk

1 tablespoon balsamic vinegar

15 ounces frozen mango, partially thawed (about 3 cups)

Fresh mint leaves, for garnish

Blend the milk, sweetened condensed milk, balsamic vinegar, and a cup of the mango in a food processor. Blend until completely smooth, then pour into serving bowls. Top with remaining mango, and garnish with mint. Serve chilled or fresh.

MOSER'S MAGNIFICENT MUFFINS

SKILL LEVEL: Expert

PREP: 10 minutes

BAKING: 25 minutes

MAKES: 12 muffins

PAIRS WELL WITH:
Hot Apple Cider (page 202), a full breakfast

Moser is the muffin man, and for those who can't travel through the Dark Portal to taste his baked goods, this recipe is the next best thing.

The first time you make a batch of morning treats from this recipe, nobody will be able to deny that these are some seriously hot muffins. Warm, spiced, and iced, with a harmony of subtle flavors and textures, these muffins absolutely live up to their name.

"Yea, yea, I'm the Muffin Man. You know why? Because I sell muffins, that's why." –Muffin Man Moser, Shattrath City

1 cup milk

1 tablespoon apple cider vinegar

½ cup applesauce

½ cup packed brown sugar

⅓ cup vegetable oil

1 egg

1 teaspoon vanilla

1 teaspoon ground cinnamon

½ teaspoon ground ginger

1 cup rolled oats

2 teaspoons baking powder

½ teaspoon baking soda

Pinch of salt

2 cups all-purpose flour

1. **Preheat the oven to 350°F** and line muffin tin with 12 liners.

2. **In a medium bowl, mix together the milk, vinegar, applesauce, brown sugar, oil, egg, and vanilla,** beating to ensure everything is evenly mixed. Add the spices, followed by the oats, then the baking powder, baking soda, and salt. Stir in the flour 1 cup at a time until the mixture just comes together in a thick batter. Divide the batter evenly among the muffin cups.

3. **Make up the streusel topping by rubbing the butter into the dry ingredients** until there are no large pieces of butter remaining. Carefully spoon this on top of the filled muffin cups, pressing very gently to bond the two.

4. **Bake for 25 minutes,** or until the tops are slightly brown and a toothpick inserted into the muffins comes out clean. Remove from oven, allow to cool for a few minutes in the pans, then move to a wire rack to finish cooling.

Continued . . .

MOSER'S MAGNIFICENT MUFFINS (CONTINUED)

STREUSEL TOPPING

3 tablespoons unsalted butter

Pinch of salt

⅓ cup flour

⅓ cup brown sugar

1 teaspoon ground cinnamon

½ cup rolled oats

MAPLE-NUTMEG ICING

1 cup confectioners' sugar

Dash of vanilla

Pinch of ground nutmeg

2 teaspoons pure maple syrup

2 to 3 tablespoons milk

5. While you wait, make up the icing: Combine the confectioners' sugar, vanilla, nutmeg, and maple syrup in a small bowl. Gradually begin adding the milk until you have a thick but workable consistency. Drizzle this over the cooled muffins and enjoy!

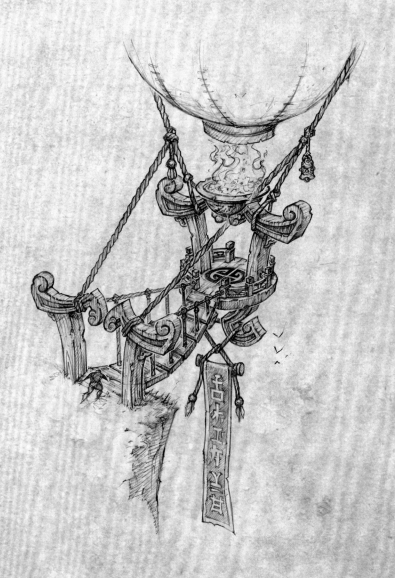

POMFRUIT SLICES

SKILL LEVEL: Expert

PREP: 10 minutes

COOKING: 20 minutes

MAKES: 2 to 4 servings

PAIRS WELL WITH: Hot Apple Cider (page 202), pork or chicken dishes

Found only in the Vale of Eternal Blossoms, these Pomfruit Slices are a delicious mix of sweet and sour. Known to increase agility, this dessert will make you feel as light as a feather.

2 medium Granny Smith apples, cored, peeled, and cut into rings or wedges

Vegetable oil for frying

BATTER

¾ cup flour

2 tablespoons cornstarch

¾ teaspoon baking powder

1 tablespoon sugar

½ cup fizzy cider

CARAMEL COATING

⅔ cup honey

1 tablespoon granulated sugar

⅔ cup heavy cream

1 teaspoon unsalted butter

A generous pinch of Ancient Pandaren Spices (page 17)

1. **Heat about an inch of oil in a small frying pan over medium heat.** In a separate bowl, whisk together the ingredients for the batter. Gently dip one piece of apple into the batter, letting the excess drip off before lowering into the hot oil. Fry for about a minute on each side, or until it is golden brown and puffy. Remove to a plate lined with paper towels to drain, and pat dry on top as well. Repeat with all apples.

2. **When the apples are done, make your caramel sauce.** Combine the honey, sugar, and heavy cream in a small saucepan over medium-high heat. Occasionally whisk together until the mixture reaches the soft-ball stage, about 240°F. Remove from heat, and whisk in the butter and spices. If your caramel starts to separate, whisk in a splash of boiling water.

3. **To serve, plate the apple slices** and drizzle the caramel over top.

PUMPKIN PIE

SKILL LEVEL: Expert

PREP: 20 minutes

BAKING: About 1 hour

MAKES: 1 pie

PAIRS WELL WITH: Vanilla ice cream, Slow-Roasted Turkey (page 141), Winter Veil Eggnog (page 210)

What Pilgrim's Bounty celebration could be complete without a wonderful slice of Pumpkin Pie? In this recipe, right from the Bountiful Cookbook, the soft creamy texture and earthy spiced flavors are offset by a dollop of sweetened whipped cream—the crowning touch to a delicious dessert.

½ batch Flaky Pie Dough (page 22)

2 eggs

2 teaspoons Holiday Spices (page 19)

2 tablespoons finely ground almond meal

½ cup honey

One 15-ounce can pumpkin (Elwynn or Tirisfal pumpkins are best)

One 12-ounce can evaporated milk

1 batch Whipped Cream (page 21) (optional)

1. **Preheat the oven to 375°F.** Roll the Flaky Pie Dough onto a lightly floured surface to ⅛-inch thickness. Lay this sheet of dough over your pie pan, trimming the edges off. If you like, use the trimmed dough to create a decorative pattern on the crust; otherwise, just pinch the crust into a simple design.

2. **Crack the eggs into a medium bowl and beat together.** If you are using a decorative crust design, brush a little egg onto the crust to get a nice golden color, then reserve the remaining egg for the filling. Poke the bottom and sides of the pie crust with a fork to prevent it bubbling, then pre-bake the piecrust at 375°F for about 15 minutes, until the edges of the crust are just starting to turn golden.

3. **Meanwhile, make the filling:** Combine the spices, almond meal, and honey with the eggs. Add in the pumpkin, followed by the evaporated milk, stirring gently until completely combined. Pour this mixture into the pre-baked piecrust, then return to the oven and bake for another 40 minutes, or until the filling has mostly set and the crust is a darkening golden brown. Remove from oven and allow to cool completely before slicing.

4. **Top with whipped cream,** if you like, or serve alongside a scoop of ice cream.

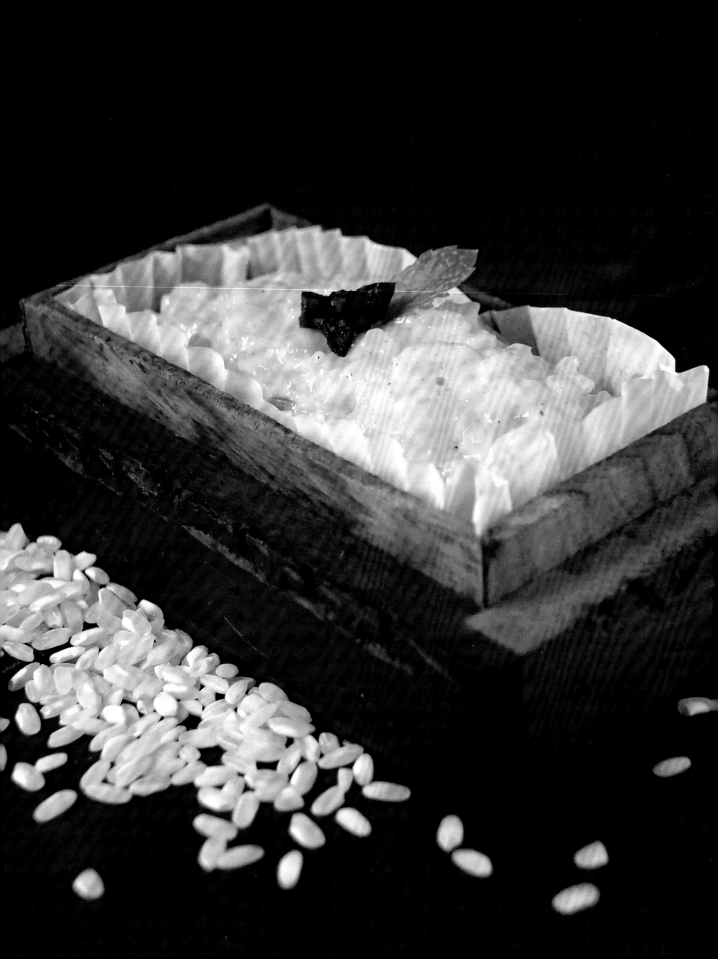

RICE PUDDING

SKILL LEVEL: Apprentice

COOKING: 30 to 40 minutes

MAKES: 4 servings

PAIRS WELL WITH:
Roasted Barley Tea
(page 208), baklava

Rice Pudding is a familiar and comforting dish across a number of cultures, so it's no great surprise to see it in Pandaria as well. Its rich and creamy texture, with slight hints of exotic spices, is just the thing for dessert or even breakfast.

This recipe comes from the Valley of the Four Winds and is a favorite of the pandaren cooking master Sungshin Ironpaw. If you want to be a Master Cook, first you'll need to perfect your Rice Pudding!

4 cups whole milk

½ cup Arborio rice

¼ cup raw sugar

½ vanilla bean, split lengthwise, seeds scraped out

1 teaspoon Ancient Pandaren Spices (page 17)

1 whole bay leaf

1. Combine all the ingredients in a medium saucepan over medium heat. Bring to a bubbling simmer, then reduce heat slightly, stirring occasionally to make sure nothing sticks. Continue to cook for about 30 minutes, or until most of the liquid has been absorbed and the rice is soft. Remove the bay leaf and discard.

This dish can be enjoyed warm or chilled.

RYLAK CLAWS

SKILL LEVEL: Master

PREP: Roughly 6 hours for dough

ASSEMBLY: 45 minutes

BAKING: 10 to 12 minutes

MAKES: About 10 claws

PAIRS WELL WITH: Robust coffee

This pastry version of Rylak Claws is infinitely preferable to being on the business end of a real rylak. Filled with a sweet, flavorful layer, each flaky "claw" is melt-in-your-mouth delicious, not to mention an impressive treat for guests!

1 batch Buttery Pastry Dough (page 23)

1 egg, beaten, for glaze

¼ cup sliced almonds

1 batch Drizzled Icing and Glaze (page 22)

FILLING

4 tablespoons softened butter

⅔ cup almond paste

½ cup granulated sugar

¼ cup brown sugar

1 tablespoon cinnamon

1. **In a small bowl, combine all the ingredients** for the filling until very smooth.

2. **Preheat the oven to 400°F.** On a lightly floured surface, roll out half the dough to a rectangle roughly 20 x 10 inches.

3. **Spread the filling evenly over the entire surface,** leaving a small gap on one long side. Gently begin rolling the dough up lengthwise, rolling toward the exposed gap of dough. Press the roll slightly flat to seal the edge.

4. **Using a sharp knife, make alternating diagonal cuts** down the length of the dough to create small wedge-shaped rolls. Place these rolls on a baking sheet lined with parchment paper, leaving at least two inches between each. To make the "toes," cut two slits in the wider end of each roll, pinching the three pieces into slightly more pointed shapes. Repeat with all the rolls, then cover lightly and let them rise in a warm place for about 30 minutes. When ready to bake, brush with the beaten egg. While the egg is still sticky, place an almond slice on the end of each "toe" to look like a claw. Bake for 10 to 12 minutes, or until the rolls are a beautiful golden color and cooked through.

Allow to cool completely, then drizzle with icing.

COOK'S NOTE: Double the ingredients here if you're planning on using all of the Buttery Pastry Dough for these Rylak Claws.

SUGAR-DUSTED CHOUX TWISTS

SKILL LEVEL: Master

PREP: 20 minutes

BAKING: 15 to 20 minutes

MAKES: About 18 twists

PAIRS WELL WITH: A fruity afternoon tea

Soft and airy, these delicate-looking pastries conceal a dollop of flavorful whipped cream. Be sure to grab a few the next time you are in Stormshield or Lunarfall.

1 cup water

1 stick salted butter

2 tablespoons sugar

1 cup flour

4 eggs

1 batch Whipped Cream (page 21)

1 batch Drizzled Icing and Glaze (page 22)

Confectioners' sugar (optional)

1. **Preheat the oven to 425°F** and line two baking sheets with parchment paper.

2. **Combine water, butter, and sugar in a saucepot over medium heat** and bring to a simmer. Add the flour and stir, cooking for another minute or so until the dough pulls away from the sides of the pan. Remove from heat.

3. **Transfer the dough into a large bowl** and let cool slightly for about 5 minutes. While mixing with a hand mixer, add in the eggs one at a time, pausing until each is fully incorporated into the dough. When finished, you should have a nice glossy batter.

4. **Transfer the mixture into a pastry bag with a large star tip.** Using a zigzag motion, pipe the pastry onto the prepared baking sheets in shapes about 3 inches long and 1 inch wide. Bake one pan at a time for 15 to 20 minutes, until the pastries are golden and slightly crispy. Remove from oven and allow to cool completely.

5. **To fill the pastries, poke two holes in the underside of each.** Carefully insert the tip of the piping bag into the holes and squeeze some whipped cream in, shifting the tip to make sure you fill each pastry end to end. Set on a cooling rack on top of a baking sheet, then dip each filled pastry in the Drizzled Icing Glaze, letting any excess drip off. Set on the rack to dry and dust with confectioners' sugar, if desired.

Serve immediately.

VERSICOLOR TREAT

SKILL LEVEL: Expert

PREP: 15 minutes

BAKING: 1½ hours

MAKES: About 2 dozen meringues

PAIRS WELL WITH: Hot cocoa

Crunchy and swirled with crimson, this sweet, beautiful treat is made and sold only by the night elves of Kalimdor, so it's a much sought-after dessert for visitors from other parts of Azeroth. One bite and you'll understand why.

3 large egg whites, at room temperature

Pinch each salt and cream of tartar

¾ cup granulated sugar

Dash of raspberry or strawberry flavoring

Red gel paste food coloring

1. **Preheat the oven to 200°F,** and line a baking sheet with parchment paper. Set a piping bag fitted with a large tip into a tall glass and using a small paintbrush, paint three vertical lines of food coloring along the inside of the bag. Set aside.

2. **In a medium bowl, whip the egg whites and cream of tartar on high speed for about a minute,** until they are loose and frothy. Reduce the speed to medium and gradually add in the sugar. Continue beating for about 7 minutes, until the mixture forms stiff peaks. Add in the fruit flavoring and beat until just mixed in. Using a large spoon, transfer the meringue mixture into the prepared piping bag, being careful not to disturb the food coloring.

3. **Using a circular motion, pipe the mix onto the parchment paper in swirly dollops** roughly 2 inches across. Bake for about 1½ hours, or until the meringues feel dry to the touch. Turn off the oven, and leave the pan in the oven to cool with the door cracked. Store cooled meringues in an airtight container.

DRINKS
THE WAY OF THE TANKARD

CACTUS APPLE SURPRISE

SKILL LEVEL: Expert

PREP: 5 minutes

MAKES: 2 servings

PAIRS WELL WITH: Dragonbreath Chili (page 97), Goblin Shortbread (page 171)

It gets mighty hot out in the Valley of Trials, but thankfully, Galgar has shared his own special take on the Cactus Apple Surprise. An inventive reimagining of the refreshing treat, this wonderfully cooling beverage is the perfect reward after a long day of raiding.

2 ounces tequila

1 ounce triple sec

½ ounce apple brandy

1 to 2 ounces prickly pear syrup

2 ounces lemonade

Mint for garnish

RIM

A pinch of chili powder

2 tablespoons coarse sugar

1. **Combine the chili powder and sugar for the rim of the glasses.** Run a lime slice around the rims, then gently dip into the sugar mixture. Fill glasses halfway with ice and set aside.

2. **Mix together all ingredients for the drink except the lemonade in a shaker,** and shake a few times to combine. Pour shaker over ice into two glasses and add the lemonade, topping up to taste.

COOK'S NOTE: If you cannot find prickly pears either whole or in syrup form, substitute raspberry or pomegranate simple syrup—it won't have the same unique flavor but should approximate the beautiful color.

CHERRY GROG

SKILL LEVEL: Apprentice

PREP: 5 minutes

MAKES: 2 servings

PAIRS WELL WITH: Goblin Shortbread (page 171)

An adventurer's health is important, whether they're exploring old ruins or forested wilderness. Sweet, tart, strong, and spicy, this beverage is a tasty way to overcome enemies.

6 ounces ginger beer

4½ ounces rum

3 ounces tart cherry juice

1½ ounces lime juice

Lime slices and/or cherries, for garnish

Fill two rocks glasses halfway with ice. Combine all ingredients except the garnish in a cocktail mixer or a pitcher, shaking or stirring to mix. Divide equally into the two glasses; garnish with cherries, lime, or both, and enjoy!

GARR'S LIMEADE

SKILL LEVEL: Apprentice

PREP: 10 minutes

CHILLING: 30 minutes

MAKES: 2 servings

PAIRS WELL WITH:
Fishy soups

Enjoyed by swashbuckling pirates looking to prevent scurvy, this basil-infused limeade is a must for both seasoned sailors and green ones!

2 cups hot water

Juice and zest from 4 large limes

Juice and zest from 1 lemon

3 tablespoons confectioners' sugar

2 sprigs fresh basil or tarragon

1 to 2 cups cold water

Ice cubes and fresh herbs to garnish

1. **In a medium bowl, combine the hot water, the lemon and lime juice and zest, and the sugar.** Stir until the sugar has dissolved, then add the basil leaves. Blend either in the bowl with a submersible blender or transfer into a stand blender. Process until there are no large pieces of leaf left and the mixture has turned a nice green color. Strain into a clean pitcher, add the remaining water, and chill for at least 30 minutes.

2. **When ready to serve, pour over glasses of ice** and garnish with fresh herbs.

GREATFATHER'S WINTER ALE

SKILL LEVEL: Master

PREP: 10 minutes

COOKING: 30 minutes

MAKES: About 8 servings

PAIRS WELL WITH: Cider doughnuts, roast pork

The Feast of Winter Veil isn't complete without a tall mug of this warming delight.

4 small apples

1 cup brown sugar

1 tablespoon ground cinnamon

1 medium orange

1 tablespoon whole cloves

Three 12-ounce bottles ale

2 to 3 pints apple cider

½ cup brandy

½ cup maple syrup

1 tablespoon Holiday Spices (page 19)

2 cinnamon sticks

6 large eggs, separated

1. **Preheat the oven to 350°F** and line a baking sheet with foil or parchment paper.

2. **Using a melon baller or a grapefruit spoon,** scoop out the core of the apples without breaking all the way through to the bottom, making a little pocket. Combine the sugar and the ground cinnamon, then divide equally among the hollowed apples. Stud the orange with the whole cloves, using a paring knife to poke holes, if needed. Place the filled apples and the orange on the prepared baking sheet, and bake for about 20 to 30 minutes, or until the apples are soft but not falling apart.

3. **While the apples bake, combine all remaining ingredients** except for the eggs in a large pot and warm over medium heat.

4. **In a bowl, beat the egg yolks for about a minute until they turn a very pale yellow.** In a separate bowl, whip the whites for several minutes until they form stiff peaks. Gently fold the yolks into the whites. While gently stirring the egg mixture, pour a cup of the hot ale into the bowl to temper the eggs. Pour the ale mixture into a punchbowl, then add in the egg mixture. Float the apples and orange on top. Serve in heat-proof mugs.

COOK'S NOTE: Some apples bake better than others; if your apples fall apart, you can still add them to the ale bowl—it'll just be a little more like applesauce!

HEARTHGLEN AMBROSIA

SKILL LEVEL: Expert

PREP: 10 minutes

MAKES: 4 servings

PAIRS WELL WITH: Sweet
Potato Bread (page
89), Goblin Shortbread
(page 171), spice cake

*Perfect for chilly autumn evenings or cold winter days, this
warming nectar comes recommended by Tirion Fordring and
the Argent Crusade. Even paladins need to put up their boots
and unwind!*

1 cup water

½ cup sugar

2 black tea bags

1 cinnamon stick

½ teaspoon ground cardamom

¼ cup maple syrup

1 pear, cored and diced

½ cup aged gin

**Combine the water, sugar, tea bags,
cinnamon stick, cardamom, and pear
in a small saucepan.** Simmer for 10
minutes, then remove from heat and
pull out the tea bags and cinnamon
stick. Add maple syrup and gin, serve
warm; teacups are ideal for this.

HONEYMINT TEA

SKILL LEVEL: Apprentice

PREP: 5 to 10 minutes

MAKES: 4 servings

PAIRS WELL WITH: Sugar-Dusted Choux Twists (page 189)

This tea bursts with minty flavor and just a touch of natural sweetness from the honey. Served warm, it's a popular drink in the cold weather of Northrend; chilled, it proves a refreshing way to beat the heat of summer.

4 cups water

½ cup fresh mint leaves

3 green tea bags

Honey, to taste

Combine the water, mint leaves, tea bags, and honey in a small saucepan and bring to a simmer over medium heat. Simmer for 5 to 10 minutes, then strain into mugs, or chill in the refrigerator during warmer months.

HOT APPLE CIDER

SKILL LEVEL: Expert

PREP: 15 minutes

MAKES: 4 to 6 servings

PAIRS WELL WITH:
    Slow-Roasted Turkey
    (page 141)

Steaming hot and flavored with an array of warm spices, a mug of this apple cider will take the chill out of your bones with just a sip.

½ gallon apple cider, still or sparkling

1 teaspoon Holiday Spices (page 19)

1 to 2 cups brandy

2 tablespoons brown sugar

Cinnamon sticks, for garnish

Orange peel, for garnish

Combine all ingredients except the garnishes in a medium pot over medium-high heat. Simmer for about ten minutes, then remove from heat and pour into heat-proof mugs. Twist the orange peel to release the oils, then garnish each mug with a cinnamon stick and peel.

COOK'S NOTE: An apple brandy is an excellent choice for this drink, although scotch, sherry, or rum will also serve.

JUNGLEVINE WINE

SKILL LEVEL: Expert

PREP: 10 minutes

SOAKING: 30 minutes

MAKES: About 10 servings

PAIRS WELL WITH: Brie and fruit jam

Fruity, fragrant, and irresistible to ogres, this strong Booty Bay wine is as dangerous as it is delicious. Plus, it makes enough to satisfy a small ship's crew, so everybody wins!

⅓ cup sugar

1 cup brandy

1 cup pomegranate juice

½ cup triple sec

2 apples, peeled, cored, and diced small

1 cup pomegranate seeds

2 oranges, sliced and cut into small wedges

1 large green apple, cored and diced

Other fruit, as desired, such as halved grapes, strawberries, or raspberries (optional)

Two 750 milliliter bottles fruity red wine

Combine the sugar, brandy, triple sec, and pomegranate juice in a large pitcher, stirring until the sugar has dissolved. Add the fruit to this mixture and allow it to sit for about 30 minutes, until it has soaked up some of the liquor. Pour the wine over and give everything a vigorous stir. This can be enjoyed over ice in the warm months of summer, or slightly warmed to ward off winter's chill.

KUNGALOOSH

SKILL LEVEL: Apprentice

PREP: 5 minutes

MAKES: 1 serving

PAIRS WELL WITH: Tracker Snacks (page 59)

If you are the type to climb the highest mountains or cross scorching deserts in search of a delicious drink, this recipe will reward your brave adventuring.

1¼ ounces vodka

1¼ ounces rum

¾ ounce Midori (melon liqueur)

1 splash cranberry juice

2 ounces pineapple juice

Orange wheel for garnish

Mix all ingredients except pineapple juice. Shake vigorously with ice. Strain over ice in highball or hurricane glass. Top with pineapple juice, and garnish with orange wheel.

MOONGLOW

SKILL LEVEL: Apprentice

PREP: 5 minutes

MAKES: 1 serving

PAIRS WELL WITH:
  Forest Strider
  Drumsticks (page 125)

The druids of the Moonglade know how to party. This sweet, easy-to-mix drink is a must-have for those looking to celebrate the Lunar Festival.

1½ ounces vodka

1½ ounces elderflower liqueur

1½ ounces blueberry juice

1½ ounces tonic water

½ ounce simple syrup, to taste

Combine all ingredients except the tonic water in a shaker and shake together vigorously. Strain into a tall glass filled with ice, and top off with tonic.

COOK'S NOTE: To reveal the hidden properties of this drink, put it in front of a UV light.

PANDAREN PLUM WINE

SKILL LEVEL: Apprentice

PREP: 5 minutes

MAKES: 2 servings

PAIRS WELL WITH:
Wildfowl Ginseng Soup
(page 111), fresh fruit

*The fruit! The fizz! Drink too much of this shtuff and even
Jogu the Drunk will start to sound shober to you.*

1½ ounces sake

1½ ounces orange liqueur

1 tablespoon plum jam

½ cup ice cubes

Chilled prosecco or champagne, to
taste

**Combine the sake, orange liqueur,
jam, and ice in a cocktail shaker.**
Give it a few brisk shakes, then strain
evenly into two delicate glasses. Top off
with prosecco, and enjoy!

PEARL MILK TEA

SKILL LEVEL: Master

PREP: 5 minutes

COOKING: 30 minutes

CHILLING: 1 hour

MAKES: 2 servings

PAIRS WELL WITH: Red Bean Buns (page 85)

Lightly sweetened milk tea is the base mixture in this refreshing beverage. With chewy, honey-flavored pearls at the bottom, it's halfway to a meal for a human, although it's just a satisfying snack for someone with the appetite of a pandaren.

MAKE THE TEA: Pour four cups boiling water over the tea of your choice and allow to steep for about 6 minutes. Remove the teabags, stir in the milks, and chill.

MAKE THE HONEY SYRUP: Combine the sugar and honey with one cup water in a small saucepan and bring to a boil. When the sugar has dissolved, leaving you with a thick syrup, remove from heat. Add the boba pearls to this mixture, and let them soak for at least an hour while the tea is chilling.

When you are ready to make the drink, add the chilled tea-milk mixture and a few ice cubes to a cocktail shaker or a tightly sealed jar and shake until everything is mixed. Add several generous scoops of the boba pearls to two glasses, then pour the tea mixture over. Serve with long spoons or wide straws.

COOK'S NOTE: The cooked boba should be enjoyed within three hours of cooking. If you like your tea sweeter, add some of the honey syrup to taste.

5 cups water

5 tea bags (green, black, jasmine, chai, oolong, or your favorite)

½ cup sweetened condensed milk

½ cup milk (yak milk is best, but cow's milk will work)

½ cup raw sugar

½ cup honey

1 cup cooked boba pearls, made according to packaging

ROASTED BARLEY TEA

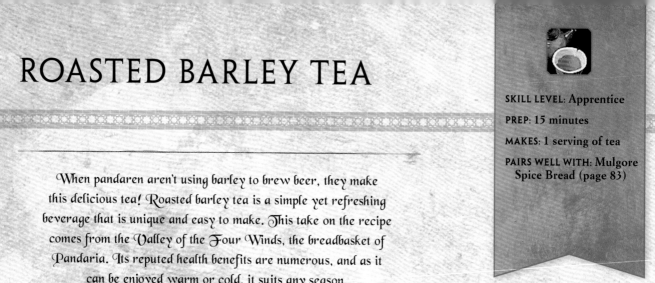

SKILL LEVEL: Apprentice

PREP: 15 minutes

MAKES: 1 serving of tea

PAIRS WELL WITH: Mulgore
Spice Bread (page 83)

When pandaren aren't using barley to brew beer, they make this delicious tea! Roasted barley tea is a simple yet refreshing beverage that is unique and easy to make. This take on the recipe comes from the Valley of the Four Winds, the breadbasket of Pandaria. Its reputed health benefits are numerous, and as it can be enjoyed warm or cold, it suits any season.

¼ cup pearl barley

1½ cups boiling water

Honey, to taste

1. **Begin by roasting your barley:** Pour the barley grains into a dry skillet over medium-low heat, and gently begin to toast it. Stir the barley every once in a while to prevent burning and to ensure that all the grains are relatively evenly toasted. When the barley is a nice golden brown, remove from heat.

2. **Steep the barley in the boiling water for about 5 minutes.** Sweeten with honey, if you like, or drink plain.

3. **This recipe can be increased to serve more people** or to make a larger pot of tea that can be chilled and enjoyed later. Store extra roasted barley in an airtight container.

SOUTH ISLAND ICED TEA

SKILL LEVEL: Apprentice

PREP: 5 minutes

MAKES: 1 strong serving

PAIRS WELL WITH:
Skewered Peanut
Chicken (page 139)

*Sad about the Cataclysm? Not after one of these.
The pineapple puts a joyful new spin on an old classic.*

½ ounce golden rum

½ ounce gin

½ ounce vodka

½ ounce tequila

½ ounce triple sec

1 ounce sour mix

Pineapple soda

**Combine the spirits and sour mix
in a shaker and shake vigorously for
several seconds.** Serve in a tall glass
over ice, and top up with the soda.

WINTER VEIL EGGNOG

SKILL LEVEL: Master

COOKING: 10 to 15 minutes

MAKES: 6 to 8 servings

PAIRS WELL WITH: Gingerbread Cookies (page 169)

This lightly spiked concoction is Greatfather Winter's favorite beverage to help wash down all those Gingerbread Cookies.

3 cups whole milk

1 cup sugar

6 medium-sized eggs

2 cups heavy cream

1½ teaspoons vanilla

¼ cup rum

¼ cup brandy

Freshly grated nutmeg

Combine the milk and sugar in a large saucepan. Whisk in the eggs as you heat the mixture over medium heat. Cook for 10 to 15 minutes, whisking all the while, until the mixture has thickened appreciably. Remove from heat and strain into a clean pitcher or bowl. Add the cream, vanilla, rum, and brandy. Chill until ready to serve, a few days at most. Grate a little nutmeg over each glass, and enjoy!

THE IMPORTANCE OF FEASTING

Food can be almost magical in the way it brings people together. Because of this, feasts are not only a way to buff your party before an important raid, but they're also an important social staple in the world of Azeroth. They are a time to gather together with strangers and celebrate the bountiful harvest, share cookies with Greatfather Winter, or compete to find the most eggs during Noblegarden.

Most of the feasts and festivals in *World of Warcraft* have real world equivalents, so it's easy to pick your favorite in-game recipes and sneak them into a family gathering. These recipes are as versatile as they are tasty: Need to make an impression on someone you are courting? Nothing says "I love you" quite like a Delicious Chocolate Cake. Perhaps you and your

guild mates are gathering outside of Azeroth for a night of board games and beer—why not add some Buzzard Bites or Stuffed Lushrooms to the mix? Or, if you are feeling ambitious, replace the entire Thanksgiving meal with Pilgrim's Bounty dishes. Whichever is the case, the Cranberry Chutney will be a welcome addition to any table.

In short, there's something in this book for everyone. These lists are simply a starting point for putting together a feast of your own. The suggested pairings that accompany each recipe are meant to help round out a single dish into a whole meal. Feel free to mix and match, innovate, and change things to your heart's content, until you have created a feast that is as full of magic and camaraderie as any in Azeroth.

AZEROTHIAN FEASTS

BREWFEST

Celebrated by both the Horde and the Alliance, Brewfest is a time to enjoy the fermented fruits of the harvest: pretzels, cheese, and booze! The competing breweries Thunderbrew, Barleybrew, and Gordok all come together outside of the major cities in a bid to outdo each other with their special ales, meads, and beers. Brave adventurers are invited to sit back, take a pull, and sample the finest wares these brewers have to offer.

- **Cheddar-Beer Dip**
- **Essential Brewfest Pretzels**

HALLOW'S END – HALLOWEEN

Hallow's End promises tricks, treats, and triumphs for boys and ghouls all across Azeroth. Each year, you'll find a special Hallow's End Wickerman set up and ready to burn in Stormwind and near the Undercity within the ruins of Lordaeron. Every four hours, Genn Greymane and Lady Sylvanas will arrive to light each faction's respective Wickerman in celebration of Hallow's End. Of course, it wouldn't be Hallow's End without a little mischief . . .

- **Fel Eggs and Ham**

PILGRIM'S BOUNTY – THANKSGIVING

Pilgrim's Bounty is a festival of food and sharing and can be celebrated outside of each of the major cities. There, adventurers will find feasting tables full of wonderful seasonal cuisine, which they can gorge on themselves or share with others—if they're feeling generous.

- **Candied Sweet Potatoes**
- **Cranberry Chutney**
- **Slow-Roasted Turkey**
- **Spice Bread Stuffing**

FEAST OF WINTER VEIL – CHRISTMAS/NEW YEAR'S

The Feast of Winter Veil is a festive time of year during which adventurers can sample delicious festive treats, playfully toss snowballs, and receive special holiday gifts.

Vendors from Smokywood Pastures are available in many of the major cities to sell the most delicious dishes of the season, or you can pick up the ingredients to make your own.

- **Gingerbread Cookies**
- **Graccu's Homemade Meat Pie**
- **Graccu's Mincemeat Fruitcake**
- **Greatfather's Winter Ale**
- **Hot Apple Cider**
- **Winter Veil Eggnog**
- **Winter Veil Roast**

"LOVE IS IN THE AIR" – VALENTINE'S DAY

- **Chocolate Celebration Cake**
- **Delicious Chocolate Cake**
- **Pandaren Plum Wine**
- **Tender Shoveltusk Steak**

DARKMOON FAIRE

The Darkmoon Faire showcases the weird and the extraordinary. Gathering the exotic from around the world, Silas Darkmoon presents the Darkmoon Faire as a celebration of the wonders and mysteries found in Azeroth. The faire spends most of its time in parts unknown but is available from time to time by accessing portals in Elwynn Forest and Mulgore.

- **Forest Strider Drumsticks**
- **Spiced Beef Jerky**

PIRATES' DAY

On Pirates' Day, commoners outfitted as scurvy pirates appear in all the world's cities bringing the news that the Dread Captain DeMeza and her crew have landed in Booty Bay. If you're brave enough to share her grog, you may have what it takes to become an honorary crew member for the day.

- **Boiled Clams**
- **Cherry Grog**
- **Savory Deviate Delight**

DIETARY INFORMATION CHART

V = Vegetarian V+ = Vegan
GF = Gluten-free V* & GF* = Easily made vegetarian or gluten-free with simple alterations

Dish	V	V+	GF
Ancient Pandaren Spices	V	V+	GF
Autumnal Herbs	V	V+	GF
Bean Soup	V*		GF
Beer-Basted Boar Ribs			GF*
Bloodberry Tart	V		
Boiled Clams			GF*
Buttery Pastry Dough	V		
Buttery Wheat Rolls	V		
Buzzard Bites			GF
Cactus Apple Surprise	V	V+	GF
Candied Sweet Potato	V		GF
Cheery Cherry Pie	V		
Cherry Grog	V	V+	GF
Chocolate Celebration Cake	V		GF*
Chocolate Cookies	V		
Clam Chowder			
Conjured Croissants	V		
Conjured Mana Buns	V		
Conjured Mana Strudel	V		
Cornmeal Biscuits	V		
Crab Cakes			GF*
Cranberry Chutney	V	V+	GF
Crispy Bat Wings			
Crusty Flatbread	V		
Dalaran Brownie	V		
Deep-Fried Plantains	V	V+	GF
Delicious Chocolate Cake	V		
Dirge's Kickin' Chimaerok Chops			GF
Dragonbreath Chili			GF
Essential Brewfest Pretzels	V	V+	
Fel Eggs and Ham			GF
Firecracker Salmon			GF
Flaky Pie Dough	V		
Forest Strider Drumsticks			GF
Frybread	V		
Garr's Limeade	V	V+	GF
Gingerbread Cookie	V		
Goblin Shortbread	V		
Golden Carp Consommé			
Graccu's Homemade Meat Pie			
Graccu's Mincemeat Fruitcake			
Greatfather's Winter Ale	V		
Hearthglen Ambrosia	V	V+	GF
Herb-Baked Eggs	V		GF
Holiday Spices	V	V+	GF
Honey Bread	V		
Honey-Spiced Lichen	V	V+	GF
Honeymint Tea	V	V+	GF
Hot Apple Cider	V	V+	GF
Ironforge Rations			GF*
Junglevine Wine			
Kaldorei Pine Nut Bread			
Kungaloosh	V*	V+	
Lukewarm Yak Roast Broth			
Mango Ice	V		GF
Moonglow	V	V+	GF
Moser's Magnificent Muffin	V		
Mulgore Spice Bread	V		
Northern Spices	V		GF
Ogri'la Chicken Fingers			GF*
Pandaren Plum Wine	V	V+	
Pearl Milk Tea	V		GF
Pomfruit Slices	V		
Pumpkin Pie (with honey)	V		
Red Bean Buns	V		
Rice Pudding (rice, yak milk)	V		GF
Roasted Barley Tea	V	V+	
Roasted Quail			GF
Rylak Claws	V		
Sautéed Carrots			GF
Savory Deviate Delight			GF*
Skewered Peanut Chicken			GF
Sliced Zangar Buttons	V*		GF
Soft Banana Bread	V		
Sour Goat Cheese	V		GF
South Island Iced Tea	V*	V+	
Spice Bread Stuffing	V		
Spiced Beef Jerky			GF
Spiced Blossom Soup	V*		GF
Spicy Vegetable Chips	V*	V+	GF
Steaming Chicken Soup			
Steaming Goat Noodles			GF*
Stuffed Lushrooms			GF*
Sugar-Dusted Choux Twists	V		
Sweet Potato Bread	V		
Tender Shoveltusk Steak			GF
Tracker Snacks			GF
Versicolor Treat	V		GF
Westfall Stew			
Whipped Cream	V		GF
Wild Rice Cakes	V		
Wildfowl Ginseng Soup			GF
Winter Veil Eggnog	V		GF
Winter Veil Roast			GF
Yu-Ping Soup			GF

**INSIGHT
EDITIONS**

PO Box 3088
San Rafael, CA 94912
www.insighteditions.com

f Find us on Facebook: www.facebook.com/InsightEditions
🐦 Follow us on Twitter: @insighteditions

Library of Congress Cataloging-in-Publication Data available.

ISBN: 978-1-60887-804-8

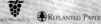 🍇 REPLANTED PAPER

Insight Editions, in association with Roots of Peace, will plant two trees for each tree used in the manufacturing of this book. Roots of Peace is an internationally renowned humanitarian organization dedicated to eradicating land mines worldwide and converting war-torn lands into productive farms and wildlife habitats. Roots of Peace will plant two million fruit and nut trees in Afghanistan and provide farmers there with the skills and support necessary for sustainable land use.

Manufactured in China by Insight Editions

10 9 8 7 6 5 4 3 2 1

INSIGHT EDITIONS

Publisher: Raoul Goff
Art Director: Chrissy Kwasnik
Designers: Malea Clark-Nicholson and Brie Brewer
Executive Editor: Vanessa Lopez
Associate Editors: Greg Solano and Courtney Andersson
Editorial Assistant: Warren Buchanan
Production and Editorial Manager: Alan Kaplan
Production Editor: Elaine Ou
Production Manager: Alix Nicholaeff
Production Assistant: Sylvester Vang

BLIZZARD ENTERTAINMENT

Blizzard Director of Story and Creative Development: James Waugh
Lead Editor, Publishing: Robert Simpson
Senior Editor: Cate Gary
Art Editor: Logan Lubera
Producers: Jeffrey Wong, Rachel de Jong
Senior Manager, Global Licensing: Byron Parnell

Special Thanks
Dana Bishop, Sean Copeland, Evelyn Fredericksen, Frank Mummert, Justin Parker, Joanna Perez

www.blizzard.com